VIA Folios 148

Books by Vincent Panella

The Other Side

Cutter's Island

Lost Hearts

Sicilian Dreams

© 2020, Vincent Panella

Cover design by James F. Brisson
Cover photo: *Mulberry St., New York, N.Y.* from Detroit Publishing Co.,
   Library of Congress

Library of Congress Control Number: 2020938578

Printed in the United States.

Published by
BORDIGHERA PRESS
John D. Calandra Italian American Institute
25 W. 43rd Street, 17th Floor
New York, NY 10036

VIA FOLIOS 148
ISBN 978-1-59954-156-3

Sicilian Dreams

Vincent Panella

Vincent Panella
4813 Augur Hole Road
South Newfane, VT 05351

BORDIGHERA PRESS

For Susan Sichel

And banished from man's life his happiest life,
Simplicity and spotless innocence!

Paradise Lost

CHAPTER 1

It started with music, happy and wild, as if played by children—sliding trumpet notes, irregular drumbeats, blasts from a tuba. From the lower valleys musicians led the parade up the switchbacks with the demonstrators close behind. One of the vanguard on a galloping mule stopped and told Santo that the *Fasci* league from the neighbor town was coming.

"We've won!" he cried as his mule danced on the stones. "We've won a great victory! You're next in the struggle! Come up to town, where Don Vito Cascio Ferro will speak to you!"

"Will this man give us work? Will he feed our families?" Santo asked, standing at the gate of his house downhill from the town wall. He was tall and clean shaven, dressed in black trousers and a shirt buttoned at the neck. He waved his hand in disbelief and said, "We've seen this before."

"Not with Don Vito on our side. His words will feed families as well as minds," said the messenger. He spoke with a *palermitano* accent. "For ten years I worked in the sulfur mines. Six days a week and still there wasn't enough to eat! Then the *Fasci* showed us how to change our lives. Come and listen to Don Vito's message!"

Santo heard another blast of music. Around the last switchback came the parade, led by a small boy with a bass drum strapped to his back. A drummer walked behind him, beating loud and slow, beating to set the pace. Horns and bells followed in rhythm and tune, then the people. Peasant men in black caps rode sidesaddle on their donkeys, women in gay bandannas were packed into painted carts. Those on foot held flying gonfalons showing religious coats of arms; others, sweating with their labor, carried teetering statues of saints or banners proclaiming the victory of peasants over landowners. Last came a red and yellow cart painted with figures from Sicilian myth and pulled by two mules in elaborate harness. Standing in the cart and reaching down to touch the hands of spectators was a tall man with a long gray beard.

Santo followed the parade. Don Vito's cart drew up in the piazza next to the statues of Peter and Paul.

"What is property?" Don Vito asked, scanning the crowd. His long beard made him look ascetic, even haunted. Gripping the cart rail tightly to dramatize his message, he continued. "Property is an idea, nothing more. It's like the air, for the use of all humanity. Is the air for sale? Does one buy air as one might buy a pair of shoes made with the hands! No, property is in the imagination! Ownership can be traced to those who stole the property long before men kept records. Who owned the land then? All of us! Property, my friends, is thievery!"

Don Vito's words were a revelation, and they struck Santo's heart with a fearful challenge. Nobody had ever suggested such an idea in this place before. Speaking against the system in Castellano was worse than blasphemy. God could be challenged, but the men who ruled over Castellano controlled bodies, not souls. They were the land managers, men who exerted control by force. Now these men were being exposed by their economic superior and social equal. Don Vito Cascio Ferro was a landowner born into nobility. He was also a man with a criminal past. Some said his interest in the movement was a cover for his crimes, which ranged from animal theft to murder and kidnapping. Many said that politics was his amusement.

Don Vito's first political act had been to give up his land. He leased it to the peasants in his town, free. Then he joined the *Fasci* and marched against factory owners in Palermo for better working conditions. These demonstrations often ended in violent clashes between workers and police. Now the *Fasci Siciliani* were moving into the countryside. They were challenging the way rural Sicilians had lived for centuries. Under this system landless peasants worked for corrupt land managers, not for land owners. The *Fasci* wanted the managers eliminated. They wanted peasants to work directly for the landowners. They wanted the greatest landowner, the church, to surrender land so peasants could buy it.

The *Fasci* on parade had just leased the land in their town directly from the owners. There were no longer managers to cheat the peasants of their commissions. The new crop share was 40 percent with no hidden costs and no secret payments for the "right to work." Now the *Fasci* wanted the Castellanese to do the same.

"You must help one another to eliminate these managers," said Don Vito.

His attention was directed toward Santo, also a tall man, who stood head and shoulders above the crowd.

"I see strong men among you," he continued. "I see men willing to work for the good of all. Tell the barons who own the land that you'll no longer work for their corrupt managers. Tell them you'll no longer break your bones for a handful of beans and a few loaves of bread, for the sick animals in the herds you fatten! Tell them you'll no longer sacrifice three-fourths of the cheese you produce and which goes into their bellies while your children shrink from hunger!"

When the speech was finished he stepped down from the cart, drank some water, and shook the hands of those who crowded around. But all the while he shot glances at Santo, who returned his looks.

"I want to meet this man," said Don Vito as he came up to Santo.

The two men were the same height. They were equally gaunt. Don Vito's dark, expressive eyes looked directly at Santo. They flickered and stopped, as if pausing to make a record of what he saw.

He touched Santo's arm and drew him closer.

"A little older and you could be my twin. You aren't like the others. I can tell by the way you hold yourself and look at me directly. You aren't interested only in yourself. But you could work for others and gain a great deal in the process."

His eyes were still riveted on Santo. His beard was patched with black, and his hair lay in grizzled swatches of varied length as if cut with dull shears.

Don Vito continued. "We need a *Fascio* here, a league of men to win leases on the Castellano estates. Will you turn away, or will you be a man and improve your lot? I tell you now, within five years most of the men around you will be in L'America, and Sicily will be left to those with the foresight to see its future."

"A future without young men," answered Santo skeptically, feeling confident as he stepped closer to meet Don Vito on his own terms. "What kind of future when they will all be in L'America? They know that one man, or even a few, can't change conditions here. When you leave here today the Castellanese will forget."

Don Vito blinked several times, as if his speech were blocked at the mouth and trying to come out of his eyes. Santo felt the press of the crowd around him. Men had gathered to hear a debate.

Don Vito waited for the audience to build, then he spoke.

"The first condition for change is patience. Don't mock those who are slow to absorb new ideas. This has been a life of defeat, especially in Sicily, which has been without a historical clock for centuries."

Santo wanted to know exactly how a peasants' league was formed. He wanted to test this great Don Vito. But before he could speak, the church bells clanged and cries of "*carabinieri!*" blew up from the crowd like a gust of wind. Like a giant caterpillar engulfed in dust, a force of police was marching up the switchbacks from the valley below.

With a shuffle of horses and a barked command an advance squad of police now approached the piazza. A mounted lieutenant entered the square through a portal. He held his horse to a slow walk and kept one hand on his cap while bending under the archway. Once in the open he dismounted, gave the reins to an aide, then called out, "Don Vito Cascio Ferro!"

The crowd now opened a path between the two men. The lieutenant paused, then started forward as the crowd cheered. He saluted Don Vito and said that a larger force was coming soon. They would disperse the *Fasci* by any means. The lieutenant respectfully asked that Don Vito leave before the force arrived. It was led by a captain with less sympathy for this cause than himself.

Don Vito reassured the lieutenant that he would leave in time, then returned to the cart and continued to speak. Without urgency, he introduced other speakers, all with the same message. During the speeches, men brought news of the column's progress, at times pleading with Don Vito to start the march back home. Don Vito waited until the column came up and around the last switchback. Then he jumped onto the cart and waved one hand in a circle. The *Fasci* raised their saints and banners and blew their trumpets. The drumming resumed, and the parade started downhill in the opposite direction from the approaching column. At the last minute Don Vito called Santo to him, and holding his beard away from the turning cart wheel, he said,

"Remember, patience and humility!"

At that moment, despite his cynicism, Santo believed change was possible. He'd been drawn to something logical by a man with whom he felt a strong affinity. Don Vito was a thinking man, one who could see the future. It was here, in Sicily.

He thought about Don Vito's advice. Would those who remained behind prosper? He was surrounded by patience and humility, and Don Vito had sensed how much patience and humility Santo had of his own. What kept him in Sicily? A house and a shovelful of land? A mother whose life was a path between home and church, and who wouldn't even hear of L'America? Or was it the image of his father, who walked the streets like a ghost, a bag of bones in a black suit, railing at the ignorance of his fellows.

Santo had watched his son, Franco, earn a few lire by cutting hay and wild fennel, anything edible for man or beast which grew along the roadsides, the only property that belonged to Sicilians by law. Such was as far as the boy would rise. He saw his daughter, Mariana, in the same gray smock she'd worn for years, her maturing body pushing against the fabric. What was in Sicily for her? A no-good like Nicolo Infante already promised to another woman and sniffing around her like a dog? Some other defeated man with nothing to offer?

Santo Regina was a widower of thirty-two, still living with his wife's ghost, which, like his father's, performed before his eyes the repetitive woman's work, changing dough into bread and pasta, stirring pots of boiling water, squeezing the dirt from laundry, shelling peas, preserving vegetables, the endless road of handwork that sometimes made death seem a blessing.

Patience and humility. Day after day Santo rode to his postage stamp of land with a *zappa* and furrowed his beans and squash and tomatoes. He began to speak to those men he met on the way. He asked them if they were happy with their lot. And he discovered it was impossible to know what these men believed. In the same conversation a man would call the *Fasci* troublemakers and then agree with everything they stood for. A man could become excited over prices for seed or tools or animals yet become completely dumb when presented with Don Vito's leveling ideas about property. Even more surprising, most men seemed not to care about the middlemen to whom they paid unfair commissions. To them the only issue was work. They would take it for any price, even subsistence wages. And if they had the money, they would even pay for work. And in the course of this thinking and talking, throughout the summer, when the crops grew and the harvest began, Santo found few men willing to join a peasants' league.

He passed the largest estate in the Castellano district and saw the harvest piled up around the barns: mountains of broad beans and hills of golden wheat ready to be threshed. There were carpets of sheep, bunches of black cattle solid as rocks. There were donkeys, mules, and horses. There were families of peasants to service this great accumulation.

The owner of this estate was a baron living in Palermo. All landowners were called barons. The property manager was the more important man: he leased the estate from the owner and hired the peasants. His name was Giuseppe Cassino, and he was so powerful that on the day of the *Fasci* march he placed armed men at the entrance to the estate, daring the crowd to come onto his land.

At the road to the estate, which cut through a stubbled wheat field, Santo paused. His goal had been to march down that road with fifty men behind him and announce calmly to the great Don Peppino— Cassino's title of respect—that not a single Castellanese would work for his crop rates or day wages. Then he would leave, and wait for Don Peppino to come begging.

That day he decided to march down the road alone. He started for the estate. Don Peppino's men and some of their women were threshing wheat and broad beans near the stone barns. Santo went closer. Men with pitchforks spread out the wheat mounds for threshing. They didn't look at Santo. They didn't look anywhere. Their eyes were glazed over. How were generations of men enslaved? With fear, applied over time: physical fear, spiritual fear. Fear of being hurt, fear of being scorched in the fires of hell, fear of having the soul blackened and burnt like paper. But like property, fear must be an idea. Fear had to be immaterial in order to be powerful.

The air smelled of manure and chaff dust. The peasants were

driving mules in circles through the wheat mounds. Men and women with pitchforks threw up the chaff, allowing the wind to carry it away and leave the hard kernels behind.

Don Peppino emerged from one of the barns. At his side was a field man with a shotgun at port arms. The don's straw hat was rotten around the sweatband. His eyes were shaded by the brim.

Santo felt the sun on his neck. He rubbed himself there. What did he have to lose? He spoke, and his voice seemed to come from behind him. "You must put more men to work. This land belongs to everyone."

Don Peppino was a short man. He looked up, and Santo could see his eyes widen with amazement. Santo wondered if he'd taken the man by surprise. This was luck, to succeed at the moment he was ready to give up! But when Don Peppino's expression of amazement went unabated, Santo had another idea. Perhaps Don Peppino was angry because he hadn't been properly addressed. Santo hadn't removed his hat. He hadn't used the mandatory "Don." He'd purposely omitted that expression in the new spirit of things.

In the extended silence, as the peasants working around the building moved like figures in a dream, Don Peppino began to smile, as if Santo's logic had finally sunk in.

Santo prepared to speak again; his hands came out slightly from his sides. He was ready to use his own voice. "We need work. Our families are hungry."

Near Don Peppino were some open sacks of shelled broad beans. He reached into one of the sacks and took out a handful of the hard beans, shaking them like dice, holding them near his ear as if listening to their message. "How do you speak to me?" he asked.

Don Peppino had surely seen the light. He was ready to offer those beans in the manner of a sign. Perhaps the logic had drawn him out and he was ready to joke about the matter.

"Do you forget my name?" he asked, jiggling the beans a little faster. "Do you forget who I am, or how to greet me?"

Words came to Santo's lips, then stopped. Something hit his face and fell to the ground. Don Peppino had thrown a single bean. Smiling now, he began throwing beans at Santo's feet. "There's your food," he said. He took the shotgun from his field man, clicked back the hammer, and fired.

A hot wind burned Santo's ears.

"This isn't Palermo," said Don Peppino. He reached into the sack once more and began flinging beans by the handful. "Go away!" he cried. "Here are your beans!"

Santo turned and started walking. The hard beans were hitting his clothing and the back of his neck. He prepared for the sound of the shotgun, or even a blast of pellets on his back. He focused on some pine trees at the end of the road. One tree in particular was set off by itself and dense with branches. Santo headed for the tree, it grew by itself with sun all around it. He and his family would have to live like that tree, alone.

He thought about this encounter for some time. As the news of his failure spread through Castellano he felt that other men could see through his skin and into his ineffectual bones. In Castellano the dead were living, and were the wiser for it.

Talk of a peasants' league died quickly after the incident with Don Peppino. In other parts of Sicily, the *Fasci* had drawn a strong reaction from the government. After more demonstrations and shooting battles the police were arresting the leaders as anarchists and criminals. The rumor was that Don Vito had escaped to Tunis. And for men like Santo, who'd made enemies at home, there was only one alternative: to leave the country.

CHAPTER 2

Clear in the moonlight, the road stretched to the horizon, straight on the slopes, wrinkled with switchbacks on the steeper hillsides. Mounted on his mule, Santo descended through snow-patched fields bounded by unmended stone walls and sparse vegetation. He passed among hillsides where sheep and goats had eaten last year's grass to the ground. This road would take him beyond the lower valleys, to the sea and Palermo.

He was the only one traveling downhill. The villagers returning to Castellano were coming uphill in irregular file. They sat sideways on donkeys or walked bent over like broken sticks, bearing on their heads bundles of firewood or bunches of hay tied with strips of rag.

Some passed him by as if he didn't exist. A few greeted him with a single word: "*Contrastamu.*" We are struggling. This was their view of life, muttered with the monotony of prayer at the end of the Mass. Santo, astride his mule, would raise his hand in greeting, then whisper under his breath, "You are dead men, all. And now I leave you."

Santo Regina didn't consider himself a peasant, a *contadino*, even though he identified with them. Unlike many Castellanese, he could read and write. He owned a small house. Through generations of thrift his family had managed to buy a small garden plot on mountain land where the naked peaks dropped off to rough plateaus.

Those men choosing to remain in Sicily didn't consider themselves dead. They were patient souls who played with the cards life dealt, pretending to be dumb for their own good. They knew only too well why Santo was heading down the mountain with a packed valise, a pistol strapped to his thighs, and a double-barreled *lupara* slung over his shoulder.

Farther down the hill he met a man leading a white goat to which a hoe and shovel were tied. This was a friend named Simone who took the bridle of Santo's mule and looked pointedly at the weapons. "Where the hell are you going, to war?"

"To L'America."

"L'America!" Simone said. "Then you are going to war. You didn't get enough trouble here so you're looking for more."

"There's no trouble where I'm going. There's no trouble in L'America."

"That's what you think! Trouble doesn't lie in the place, but with the men. There would have been no trouble here either, but you became a politician."

Santo didn't want to argue the point. He looked up and down the hill, at the fragile trail of peasants making their way back to the town.

"Should I become like these others?" he asked. "Should I walk like the dead?"

"No, but at least they walk," replied Simone.

"Listen, my friend, in L'America there is no politics. They have no time."

Simone laughed again. "Do you have work over there?"

"The steamships are full of bosses. They will give me work."

"And steal your money."

"Maybe, but maybe not."

"I see you've changed. You're more resigned."

"The days of Don Vito are over, my friend. I have a family to look after."

"Good luck, then." He released the mule's bridle, then yanked roughly on the goat he'd allowed to graze while they talked. "Watch out for those bosses. They'll feed you rotten food and cheat you out of your pay. And when they no longer need you to shovel their shit, they will send you home to shovel Sicilian shit once again."

Simone continued uphill and Santo watched the darkness swallow first him, and then the white goat. He turned his mule downhill and urged it on. Darkness had come on perhaps too fast for his purpose. At the corner of the last switchback he guided the mule into some dense brush and dismounted. He tied the animal out of sight, unslung the *lupara* and sat on a rock with the weapon cradled in his arm. With a view of the road, he examined the face of each passerby, bitterly amused because those he'd described to Simone as the walking dead gave him no more recognition than if he and his weapon were part of the stone itself. Sicilians were beaten, but they weren't stupid.

A young man sitting sideways on his donkey approached from below. He was nodding his head to the animal's gait, as if sleeping, but he wasn't sleeping. Santo stepped out and blocked the path.

The young man slid off the donkey and touched his cap in salute. He was small and unshaven.

Santo pointed the *lupara* at his chest and spoke his name. "Infante, Nicolo."

"Yes, sir."

"I'm going to L'America."

Nicolo looked at Santo briefly, then turned his face to the dark sky, as if the weather wouldn't be favorable for such a trip. Then he looked back and squinted. "Why do you tell me this?"

"Why do you pretend to be dumb?"

Nicolo exhaled loudly, then rolled his eyes to turn himself into the injured party. Santo pulled back both hammers of the *lupara* and shoved it into Nicolo's chest. The young man looked around as if he could plead his case to the empty road. Santo said, "Look at me!" and grasped Nicolo's shirt collar. He pushed the *lupara* muzzle under his nose. Nicolo backed away and tried to speak, but all that came out was his breath coming short.

"When you pass my house, do you make signs to my daughter? Do you have words with her?"

"It means nothing! It's courtesy, just courtesy! I'm already promised to someone else."

Santo stepped back. "I'm going away but not for long, and I leave behind my one treasure, the only jewel in my life. She's younger than she looks. She's not as old as she might try to behave. Do I need to say more?"

Nicolo shook his head up and down and Santo gestured toward his donkey. "Now get on top of your true *signorina* and remember, I'll return sooner than you think."

He kept the weapon pointed while Nicolo boosted himself onto the donkey and shook the lead. The animal stepped off briskly. Santo waited for a moment, then returned to the rock where he'd been sitting. He put the weapon away and spat several times to calm himself.

When Nicolo disappeared into the darkness, Santo mounted and continued downhill. The regular step of the mule echoed back from the rocks as he kicked the animal into a canter. In this year of 1907, Santo Regina was joining the tide of history, when over a quarter million Italians would emigrate to L'America. Most were from the south, like himself, and the growing United States had a specific hunger for these poor Italians, mostly from rural areas. Some would remain. Others, called "swallows," or "birds of passage," would work seasonally on farms, in mines, or on construction crews. They would then return home, often to repeat the pattern. After a few such trips, Santo could seal up his house, and with son and daughter in hand take the steamship to New York, where his sister had already started a life.

He kept his pace until the mule began to blow: then he slowed to a walk. By morning he would be in Palermo. The mule and his weapons would stay with a cousin. He would go to L'America with a folding knife for eating and extra money sewn into his jacket. He would be one more bird in the flock, anonymous, humble, and patient.

CHAPTER 3

Mariana awoke. Her grandmother—Nonna—sat on the bed and fixed her with small, liquid eyes as her lips moved in prayer. Some withered beauty marks sprouting single hairs marked the old woman's face. She prayed the rosary with a barely audible whisper as she raised two hands bound with beads and a crucifix. She gestured toward town. She was going to Mass.

Mariana waited until Nonna went out the front door, then she rose and washed from a basin, pressing cold water into her eyes and running wet hands through her long, dark hair.

She ate some bread dipped into coffee heated with milk and sugar. Then she took a dusting rag and a stick broom and climbed the ladder to a small room with a slanted ceiling made of timbers laid over with roof slates. Sunlight leaked through the slates. This was her father's bedroom, the father gone across the ocean to work. The room had a small bed, and at its foot a pressboard trunk with her mother's most valuable clothing and handmades, which would someday belong to her. Long, rusty spikes mortared into the walls held her father's things: woolen caps, a winter coat, shoes hung by the laces, a pistol smeared with Cosmoline. These items were displayed to suggest that Santo was still at home. They were also an implied warning to Mariana and her brother that he might walk in the door at any moment.

She opened a door onto the balcony but didn't step outside. She was forbidden to show herself. The balcony had a view of the road, and directly below was a small garden planted with herbs. Up the hill was the Castellano town wall, a perimeter of attached stone houses broken by an archway into the piazza. Mariana could see Nonna passing through the archway bent forward on her cane and swiveling her head to inspect her surroundings. Her destination was the Church of Saints Peter and Paul, built at the highest point in the town. Its twin domes of gold and blue mosaics were topped by iron crosses scratching at the sky.

A rooster came down the road looking for something to eat. The bird was let out every morning so its hens could lay in peace. If the rooster was not home by late afternoon, a gossip named Teresa would come after it. Old Teresa had no qualms about entering the Regina property. Once through the front gate, the old woman would imitate the bird, taking slow steps, looking around corners with one suspicious eye, and clucking with such authentic rooster sounds that Mariana, the other subject of her spying, was often deceived.

Until recently Mariana had been content to plot her life with predictable markers such as the regularity of Teresa's rooster, marriage, and the pressboard trunk with its home fittings. Then there would be children, old age, and life as a grandmother. She would be buried underground until her flesh melted into the soil. Her bones would then be dug up and cemented into the Regina vault. Her children would cross themselves in her memory each time they passed the cemetery. This was the future in a town sailing through the sky like a ghost ship. The sea of air surrounding the town was palpable, and sounds rose from the massed stonework of houses and hovered like birds: the dull, penetrating church bell, the brooding of chickens, the sound of a hammer striking stone.

But now L'America was on everyone's lips. Letters told of cities crowded with people from every part of Europe. And there were open invitations from friends and relatives to live where work was plentiful. Her aunt, Angelina, had written letters describing her *palazzo* in New York City, her relentless toil in a place where, fantastically, people paid others to bake their bread. Each letter contained a single American dollar and photographs of Angelina. She wore different clothes each time. The invitation for the family was open, and living in L'America was a dream for Mariana and her brother, Franco.

The church bell rang for morning Mass and struck Mariana so her heart fluttered. The bell was a sign, and she stepped part-way onto the balcony. She closed her eyes against a swelling emotion and listened. As if her will had produced it, the sound came, the tap-tap of hooves on packed earth. It was Nicolo, coming down from the town, sitting straight on his donkey. On the pretense of adjusting his cap he looked up as Mariana raised her hand to acknowledge him.

She ran downstairs to the pantry. The room had a tiny window looking onto the road. She saw Nicolo's head moving above the stone wall. One hand lowered his cap while his eyes searched for her. He was a picture of strength and command, but his expression was puzzled, frustrated. He wanted to see her.

She put her back to the wall near the window, sideways to him now, thrusting out her breasts. He would like her that way. The thought of his adoration weakened her knees. Now he stopped at the gate, directly in front of her!

After a furtive look around he whispered her name, "Marianuzza!" This familiar form of her name had never passed his lips before. Even in town when he lifted his hat in respect, he never even said "Mariana." Now he whispered again, "Marianuzza!" She spoke his name too, but in less than a whisper, knowing he could read her lips. Then she waved him away. They were both taking too much of a chance. Even if crazy Teresa wasn't spying on them, Nonna would see the break in the donkey track! She inspected the ground in front of the house every day. Mariana waved him away once more, urgently this time.

He shook his head to show that he didn't want to leave, even that he couldn't leave. His bold eyes seemed to consume her. He motioned down the hill. He meant the washing pool.

Yes, but not now! Not now! She knew how to tell him. A look at the sky, a circular movement of her index finger to indicate the passage of the sun.

That afternoon she waited until other women passed by with laundry bundles on their heads. Taking the family laundry, she followed them down to the pool, known as "the torrent," a wide but shallow run with a grid of flat stones and a bridge passing overhead. When Mariana arrived, the women were scrubbing their laundry on the stones.

Mariana soaked a sheet, heaved it onto a stone, and began squeezing out the dirt. She looked up and saw Nicolo stopped on the bridge.

"That rascal! Pretend you don't see him." This was an older woman named Giuseppina, her washing pool friend and a distant cousin of Nicolo's. She'd already warned Mariana against him. He belonged to a family of *mafiosi*. His father worked for a large estate and took bribes from day laborers to give them work. His brother, Carmeluzzo, had been a vicious bandit; murder and stolen livestock were his specialties. He'd been run out of Sicily by his enemies. Nicolo, left to manage the family property, was doing a bad job.

"Every week he visits the whores in Palermo," Giuseppina said, wiggling her thumb between her legs. "This is where he puts it."

Nicolo stared down at Mariana. He was smiling at Giuseppina's gesture. Mariana didn't care about these rumors. Such a man could take her away from this life of beating sheets on stones, like Giuseppina. The older woman had arms and shoulders like a man, and her large eyes had a frightened look which never left her. Mariana didn't want her life.

"How do you know he doesn't have some disease?" Giuseppina asked in a whisper.

Mariana dismissed the remark with a wave of her hand.

His eyes were directly on her. He gave her the signal: a forefinger twirled once, then a look at the sun.

"What does that mean?" asked Giuseppina.

"Stay with me," said Mariana. "I'm not allowed to be here alone. Stay with me until later."

Giuseppina shrugged and hauled some sheets up from the water. "Once I was a fool like you," she said. "I went to hell for it. That's why I have no husband now. But I know what you feel and it's hard to resist."

"Keep an eye out while I meet him."

"Don't make me watch while you go to hell."

"I promise that we'll talk, no more."

"Promise me nothing. It's what you promise him that matters."

When the sun went down, Mariana and Giuseppina took the path leading from the laundry pool to the road. At a certain point Giuseppina remained behind while Mariana went ahead and turned onto a footpath through the woods to another point on the riverbank.

She came back shortly and told Giuseppina that Nicolo was waiting.

"Hurry," said Giuseppina, waving her finger as a caution. "Do nothing but talk! And don't let go of that laundry. It's your only protection."

CHAPTER 4

The man cooking breakfast inside the railroad car had white hair and skin the color of black ink. He wore boots with the ends cut open for toe room and overalls so quilted with patches that the original garment was buried like a level of civilization. He stirred three large pots on the woodstove. Two contained cornmeal, the other weak coffee. He added water to the cornmeal as required, and when the gluey mixture bubbled he added globs of lard, fresh eggs, and handfuls of black pepper. After each handful he looked for approval from the boss, Torino, who sat on a cot lacing up his boots.

"With pepper," said Torino, "Italians will eat anything." He stood up full height to test his bones for the day. His great size, bald front, and large mismatched ears suggested an elephant. He wore clean khaki clothing and a leather belt holding a pistol and a blackjack.

Torino pushed aside a curtain separating his quarters from the rest of the car and watched the men slide from their sleeping pallets. They were a sullen lot, unshaven and bad smelling. A few grumbled in their country dialect. Some were flatulent; some covered their private parts angrily, objecting to the lack of privacy inside the car; others displayed themselves with childlike pride.

Torino tasted the cornmeal, then served himself a bowl in plain view of the men. It was barely edible, but considering his feeling toward this particular crew, he wished it were poison.

"Eat! Eat!" he cried.

After the men were served Torino went to a shed that served as a company store. On Sunday the men took a half-day's rest, and ordinarily his little store would be full of men buying tobacco, food, and even straw hats to protect themselves from the sun. But three Sundays in a row hadn't seen a single sale to this collection of Sicilian cheapskates. Torino feared that the store income, which accounted for part of his salary, would be lost.

The shed was made of barked poles and slab siding. Torino swung open the door and took a seat in the back where he couldn't easily be seen. Hanging from the inside beams were *zappe*, the short-handled hoes upon which Sicilians had built their reputation as cultivators of sugarcane and cotton. Long shelves contained tobacco, overalls, shirts, underwear, socks, shoes, and such a variety of foods that a man didn't have to eat the African's cooking, if the man was willing to pay the price. Here were tins of fish, olive oil decanted into small bottles, wedges of hard, imported cheese, barrels of wine made by local Sicilians, and preserved fruits to make a man's mouth water.

Breakfast was over, and the men were jumping down from the railroad car. Some went into the nearby brush to relieve themselves; others headed uphill toward the single outhouse and a willow grove where they could relax in the shade. A loud banging noise immediately ensued. The men were throwing rocks at the outhouse. It was a game they played, trying to get the man inside to finish quickly. Torino's warnings against it had been ignored. They would wreck the outhouse soon enough. Then they could use the bushes, like pigs.

He'd never seen such a troublesome crew. It was corrupted by city types from Palermo who were devious and hard to intimidate. To these he added a country radical named Santo Regina, who'd convinced the men to boycott the store. This was after the ledger book in which Torino recorded store sales had been stolen. The pages had been ripped out and passed around the camp. Now each man knew what deductions were coming off his pay, and all of them believed—with good cause—that Torino was cheating. There were rumors of a strike if store prices weren't changed. It was an amazing development for Sicilians, who usually worked under any conditions. Torino feared a strike most of all. He was personally responsible for a contract with the plantation owner: two hundred acres of cotton had to be cultivated within a certain time. If the Sicilians quit, the crop loss would be his responsibility.

There was no way this trouble could have been foreseen. Torino tried to hire only first-time swallows, desperate men who would settle for a few American dollars to take home. Most of the Sicilians in the camp today were from villages deep in the Madonie Mountain range. They'd never been to America before, and ordinarily such types would be like clay in his hands. But there'd been political trouble up there in the mountains. The *contadini* had fought for land reform and better crop shares. Although they'd lost, the men could see the pattern in

Sicily being repeated here.

Some of the Palermo boys came up to the shed. One of them shaded his eyes and peered inside. This was the chief instigator, named Zillo, round as a ball and hairy all over.

"Good day to you, boss! We can see you're working hard already!" He and three younger ones swaggered inside, picking up the tins of food and tobacco on display. All of them kept knives in their boots.

"How much for anchovies, boss?"

"Tobacco! How much is tobacco?"

"What do sardines bring?"

"The prices are marked," Torino said.

"We don't like these prices!"

"Then get out! Don't touch, and get out!" Torino rose up and came forward. He unbuckled the strap on his pistol. "Do you hear me?"

They swaggered off, laughing, and Torino turned his eye on another man climbing down from the railroad car: Regina, the rabble-rouser.

Torino came outside. "You! Come in here!"

Santo came forward but didn't enter.

"Why are you making trouble here? Why do you ask them to strike?"

Santo lit the stub of a Toscano cigar. "I ask them nothing. But if you want to know the truth, the men may strike unless you lower the prices and wipe our slates clean. According to the record book that came into our hands, most of us will take home half the pay you promised."

"What makes you say this?"

"I have read the pages in the book. You are charging men for things they haven't bought."

Torino pointed to the boxcar, where the cook was wrestling pots of breakfast slops onto a wheelbarrow, which he began pushing toward the hog pens. "Do you see that miserable African? Among his own kind he's considered rich because he has a job. But the countryside between here and New Orleans is a jungle filled with starving and murderous Africans, those once enslaved by the whites. I can tear up your contracts and send you away. The Africans will pick your bones and nobody will care. The law protects only the whites. We Italians are just another form of slave, whether we can read or not."

"Why do you tell me this?" asked Santo, keeping his distance.

"To let you know what you're up against. There is no choice. I have your steamship tickets. I have your entry papers. Follow my rules or you go into the jungle. And whoever survives will be jailed by the immigration."

Santo conceded this point in silence and walked up to the willow grove. The men were lying on the grass or sitting against the tree trunks in the shade. Zillo and his cousins had a willow tree to themselves. They waved him over.

"Sit with us now," said Zillo. "You're the man we need. What did this boss say to you down there?"

"What you know already. The contract we signed is worthless. We have no protection against him."

"What can we do then?"

Santo directed Zillo to look down the hill. The boss was standing outside the shed looking up at them, arms folded on his chest.

Zillo stood up and saluted the boss with an obscene gesture. Then he put both hands to his mouth and made a loud, flatulent noise. "So much for him," he said. Then after drawing the group closer, he pulled out a ledger page.

"Everything is here," he said, tapping on the page with one finger. "Our friend Regina reports that this *ladrone*, like some great artist, paints numbers next to our names. According to this page, I have bought eight tins of fish, two pieces of imported cheese, a great deal of pipe tobacco, and a cotton shirt made in the factories of L'America. Now, I don't smoke a pipe. Nor do I see this cotton shirt on my back. And I'm not the only man here to buy imaginary goods. What should we do, my friends, cut him open like a fish?"

Santo leaned back against the trunk of the willow tree and set his hat over his eyes to block the sun. He watched a swallow hover on a wind draft, than sail into one of the barns near the *palazzo* which housed the landowner, a white man who sometimes walked with Torino down the cotton rows to inspect the work. Santo remembered the slogan of Torino's recruiting agent on the steamship: "Sixty days, sixty dollars!

No hidden costs. This is guaranteed!" There were thirty days left on the contract. Leaving camp with half that money would be a miracle.

"This is like home," said Zillo. "You have men with guns who work for those who own the land. They cheat both sides."

"But here it is different," Santo said.

"How?"

"Here there is no law. There are no *carabinieri*."

"But they have Africans, everywhere. Remember how we saw them on the docks in New Orleans, miserable souls begging for food and money."

"The slaves of the whites even though they've been set free," said Santo. "We are this far above them." He held up his thumb and index finger so they were touching.

Zillo stood over Santo and tapped his foot with his own. "Regina, what's the answer?"

"We can refuse to work and leave the camp, or we can work and hope."

"We can't leave the camp. He has our tickets home!" cried one of the men.

"But we can reach New Orleans," said Zillo. "There's a community of Sicilians there. We can get anything we want. We can get work, we can get papers. The American immigration will be glad to see us go back home."

One of Zillo's cousins wanted to speak. He was a blond, blue-eyed boy with the wispy foreshadow of a beard. He raised a hand for silence. "If we were home and this man took our money, what would happen?"

"Ah, Palermo," said Zillo, making such chopping motions with his hands that his cheeks shook.

"Just so," said the boy.

Zillo looked around as if this idea were now a possibility. He pinched the boy's cheek playfully. "And then what?"

The young man smiled. His teeth were milky and glasslike. "And then we go to New Orleans."

Zillo looked at Santo as if a second discovery had been made.

"Listen to me," the young man said. "Here is a man who reaches into our pockets every day and takes our money. We'll never see this money. I've heard these *padroni* often pay wages after the workers have boarded the steamship for home. The money is passed along by someone who knows nothing. So there's nobody to answer for what's been done to you. Why not kill him now? It may make life better for those who follow us. We've already been sacrificed."

Santo picked at some mud on his shoes. "Do you kill so easily?"

The boy reached into his boot and came up with a long knife whose blade was ground to a slight curve. He drew the tip gently across his throat.

"He'll do it," said Zillo, touching Santo's foot with his own once more. "This boy can do it!"

Santo looked past his little group to the *palazzo* where the owner lived. It was a massive white house with four brick chimneys and it connected to some smaller buildings that housed Negroes and animals. There was always activity around the house, usually Negroes tending animals, hanging laundry, splitting firewood. The camp was actually a cotton factory, set in the middle of endless acres of cotton plantings, untilled fields, and woodland. Here was the same pattern of ownership as in Sicily, only the land was richer, and here the Negroes took the place of the *contadini*. Santo had seen them working in the fields, walking behind mule-drawn cultivators. Like the Sicilians at home, they walked in their sleep.

He closed his eyes and tried to shut out the talk of strikes and revenge and whether they could reach New Orleans. He'd signed on to Torino's crew with every intention of minding his own business. He'd even resigned himself to being moderately cheated, if he could return home with most of his pay. Then someone stole the ledger book and asked him to read it.

One of the men cried out, "Look at that!"

Santo sat up.

Torino was downhill talking to a group of Negroes carrying shotguns. He looked up toward the grove and gestured with a sweep of his hand. The Negroes came uphill and surrounded the willow grove, holding the guns at their chests.

The boss came into the grove and clapped his hands for attention.

"Don't go beyond these Africans! They're instructed to shoot!"

He came up to Santo and said, "Hello, my friend. Do you still want to go to New Orleans?"

"The men will decide," said Santo.

Torino cried "Get up!" and began to kick at Santo's feet. Zillo immediately jumped on Torino from behind. One of the Negroes fired in the air. Torino shook Zillo off, and in one motion pulled his blackjack and struck Zillo on the head. When Zillo didn't go down, Torino struck him on his temple. Zillo fell to his knees then, and Santo kneeled beside him, pressing a handkerchief on his temple to stop the blood flow. Santo looked up. Torino held the blackjack near his ear and jiggled it obscenely. "Don't even breathe in my direction," he said.

Zillo had a lump on his temple the size of a bird's egg. "No man does this to me," he said later to Santo and the blond boy.

"They think Sicilians are fools and dogs," the blond boy said. He flicked a thumb on his knife edge. "I can do it while he sleeps."

"He does it," said Zillo. "Then we follow the railroad to New Orleans. We can do it soon. Let him think that we now behave like good little swallows and work hard. We will buy things in his crooked little store and pretend all is forgiven."

"I can't be part of it," Santo said.

"Why not?"

"I'm not free, like you. I can't risk my family."

Zillo had raised his eyebrows as if he understood everything now. "Listen to me," he said. "I will share a secret. In New Orleans there is a friend of mine, a famous Sicilian with balls like this!" He held up two hands in the shape of great globes. "Perhaps you know of him, for he came to your part of the country during the *Fasci* strikes. His name is Don Vito Cascio Ferro, and for me he will do anything. We only have to reach New Orleans."

That night Santo lay on his pallet, not sleeping. His packed valise was his pillow. He felt himself already in motion. Just above him an air hatch was propped up with a stick. The opening had served him well and would serve him again. For many nights he'd slept with his face to the cool night air, seen the moon and stars in a hazy sky, heard the comforting wheeze of swine and the clanking of pots from the house where the Negroes worked. With the speed of thought he could rise and float into the night, sailing over moonlit fields in the flight of a saint. This opening was the door to his freedom.

He sat up, thrust the valise out of the hatch and onto the car top. Then he lifted himself part way out. It was the quiet hour, insects buzzing, the mockingbird that sang all night. There were no Negro guards at night. He pushed himself out, found the ladder, and with the valise in one hand, climbed down, one rung at a time. Then something hard struck his head from behind, hands tore him from the ladder just as he made out the shape of Torino beating him with the blackjack while the Negroes held him down.

CHAPTER 5

Nicolo called her off the path with a birdlike whistle that continued as she entered the small clearing. He leaned against a rock and held a cigar to his lips. Smoke drifted from his mouth. His donkey was nearby cropping grass. Mariana remembered a recent feast day when he held himself with the same arrogance in the archway of the church.

She kept the laundry close and said, "I can't stay! I can't be seen going home alone!"

He motioned her fears away with a chopping motion of one hand and pulled at the laundry with the other. When she came closer, but still holding the laundry, he placed the cigar carefully into a depression in the rock.

"I have something for you."

"What is it?"

"A fish," he said, holding his empty hands out like a magician about to perform a trick.

"What fish are you talking about? I see no fish."

"This is what you do to me," he said, and unbuttoning himself, proceeded to show her.

Having never observed the male part in this state of arousal, Mariana saw enough of a resemblance to a real fish to briefly warp her perception. How red and strangely out of proportion was this fish to the rest of him!

Nicolo looked down on his fish with a wonder equal to hers, as if this thing from some unknown place had surprised him. Mariana now put this sight together with Giuseppina's thumb gesture and she wondered if this big thing could fit inside her without causing great pain.

"This is how strong my love is."

"And what about those whores in Palermo? Do they also make your love strong?"

"There were no whores in Palermo."

"That's not what I've been told."

With a motion of his hand he dismissed her statement, then said, "Do you want to go to L'America?" He asked this question while stroking himself.

"Yes! I want to be rich, like my aunt."

"Then hold this in your hand."

She clutched the laundry tighter to her chest and turned her face away.

"Look at it, Marianuzza! Look what you do to me!"

"I already looked, but why should I do what you say?"

"Do it and I'll take you to L'America. Show me your love and we'll go away together."

"Do you think I'm stupid? What will you do for work when we get there? How will you make money?"

"My brother lives there. He's a butcher and will give me work. I only need to write a letter."

"Why should I believe you?"

"Because of this, because of what you do to me." He then mentioned the practical aspects of his promise, steamship fares, rents, prices, wages, knowledge that impressed her. Simultaneously he stroked himself as she turned back to the human aspect of this fish—its ability to procreate, to give pleasure—and she was surprised to feel a longing in the empty part of herself.

"Here is beautiful L'America! Here she is! Touch her and see how much she likes you!"

Mariana looked around for Giuseppina, hoping she might have followed her into the clearing to urge her home, but also hoping she was gone.

"Don't worry, we're all alone," Nicolo said.

Mariana kept her eyes on the donkey tearing up grass.

"Come and touch it," she heard Nicolo say. "Come, give me your hand."

Still turned away, she gave him her free hand. He took it, and no sooner had she touched him than he placed his hand over hers and began a rubbing action to show her how to continue.

Almost instantly, something strange and frightening took place, something she'd never seen before. Like a fountain, the male part squirted a thick liquid with a smell like soap. He pulled her tight during the squirting, holding her hand on the fish with desperation.

When his breathing subsided he tried to pull her even closer but she turned away again and took a pillowcase from the bundle to dry her hand. So that was it. That was the fish and the mystery. That was the thing she would take inside herself with an action like Giuseppina had mimed with her thumb. It didn't seem so strange and unnatural now, and Nicolo, for all his bragging about the fish, was a man who'd suddenly become a boy. Now Mariana knew her strength, but also her weakness.

CHAPTER 6

Santo found himself on a cot in the slave house. An old woman leaned over him, her skin creased with lines crosshatched on her cheeks. Gray braids crowned her head, and earrings made from chicken feathers twitched when she uttered speech which sounded like the chatter of house birds. She massaged the back of Santo's neck and pushed him back into his dreams.

He'd been dreaming, or thinking back to the beginning, to the chalky road from Castellano, to the arrival in New Orleans where one of the men threw a coin onto the pier and a pack of ragged Negroes fought for it tooth and nail; then to the plantation and the trouble with Torino; finally to his last night in the railroad car when he lay on his pallet with the air hatch above his face, the moon milky and beautiful, enjoying that beauty for a few minutes before he pulled himself up through the hatch. His thoughts ended with the panic of a final image: a loose black thread hanging from his mother's lips. Her needle drawing circles in the air. The money she'd sewn into his jacket lining.

He cried out in English, "Money!" The effort raised a pain in his ribs and he lay back down. The old woman was gone. His cot had been set up in a corner of the main room. A stack of firewood walled him off, and just beyond his feet was the fireplace, which, in an astounding display of American wealth, burned day and night.

The woman came back with a bowl of food. He held up the jacket, showing her the torn lining. She poked her finger into the hole and protested in her birdlike language. He detected some English words. The bowl found its way into his hands: a greasy broth with greens like seaweed.

He gave back the food. He couldn't eat. His money was gone.

He lay in bed with his dreams and part-dreams of his surroundings: the flicker and glow of the fire, a cast-iron pot hung over the flames, a candle burning on the wall.

Each morning Negroes dropped down from an attic hatch like bees from a hive. He recognized the guards and field workers among them. When anyone stopped at the foot of his pallet he spoke softly to ease the pain in his ribs. He told them his home was in Sicily, a place not far from Africa. He held up his hands and rubbed them together—Sicily and Africa close together—but they translated his words to mean that he was African. This generated rapid nods of condescending disbelief.

The floor of the slave house was made of logs split lengthwise and adzed flat, its surface worn from use, the cracks filled with hardened dirt. Through the spaces between the stacked firewood he saw a long table and wooden benches. The rank smell of hogs and chickens rose up through the floor as these animals slept, scratched, and rooted in the cool earth under the house.

One morning he awoke to find a Negro watching him. This one wore clean, starched overalls. When he took off his big-brimmed hat he exposed a high forehead and a wide face with a rich, chocolate complexion. His short, gray-flecked hair followed the uneven contour of his skull.

He introduced himself as William, in Italian.

"I learned your language from the Sicilians in New Orleans, where I worked for a few years."

Santo felt such a great desire to speak his own language that his heart hurt. And if William had been a Sicilian, he would have poured out his worries without regard for embarrassment. But William was a stranger, and a Negro. Could he be trusted?

"Who sent you, the boss?"

"I sent myself. You might say I'm a missionary. I didn't come to this country as a slave, like these others, but on a steamship from New York, many years ago. I'm an African who chose to be with my people."

"An idealist," said Santo, saluting. "I lost my remaining idealism in this camp." He searched William's eyes. They were the same deep, brown color as his skin. They gave less of an indication of his feelings than other, more mobile features of his face: his wide, nervous nostrils and a hesitating smile, which disappeared as quickly as it showed itself.

"I hope you keep some of your idealism. When working with the Sicilians in New Orleans I learned to mix their practicality with my idealism. I hope I taught them the reverse. Each year when the Sicilians come I meet with some of them. The main reason is to show these Negroes that other worlds and languages exist. They've lost their native speech, and so will you if you remain."

"A language I'll gladly give up. If you lived in Sicily, you'd know why. What I see here resembles life at home too well."

"But you weren't afraid to leave home, or to try leaving the camp when it didn't suit you. Your attempt inspired others. Four men have left the camp, heading for New Orleans."

"And the boss?"

"Your *padrone* is close behind, not to capture them, but to recruit more Italians. He can't afford to lose a man."

"And what will happen to me?"

"The plantation owner has no interest in holding men against their will."

"How can I return home without money?"

"The owner will pay what you earned so far and return your boat ticket, which he took from Torino. He doesn't think it best that you stay here and work. If you return to New Orleans, I can take you part of the way. There are Sicilian farmers living nearby and some are friends of mine. They'll help you along."

"And then?" asked Santo.

"From New Orleans you can go anywhere. By steamship to Florida, New York, or even Italy. By train back up to Chicago, or west to Texas where there is plenty of work in the fruit orchards."

William's remarks confirmed that L'America was big, and this made Santo feel small. He coughed to suppress his tears, not caring that William saw this sign of vulnerability. He couldn't stay in this country, not now. His mother was too old to watch the children and he was sickened by the thought of returning to Castellano with nothing, defeated by *padroni* he'd boasted would never take advantage. He was a fool, undone, like the men at home he'd belittled.

CHAPTER 7

"And if I do it . . ."

"We'll go to L'America."

"How do I know you'll keep your promise?"

"My brother is rich. In L'America they call him *boss*. He finds work for all his friends."

"Everyone knows about your brother."

"What do they know?"

"That he lived in the hills and stole mules and killed for nothing."

"Yes, he was a little crazy."

"And if he's crazy, how can you be sure he'll help us?"

"Because he's my brother." Nicolo took a blanket from the donkey and spread it on the ground. "Come," he said, patting it. "Put down the laundry. Here is L'America, right here." He touched himself. "Let her swim inside you. Do what I say and we'll go there together."

"Yes, but we must be married! You must speak with my father!"

"We'll be husband and wife in L'America. They ask no questions there."

"My father!"

"Don't worry, we'll speak. We've already spoken, in fact. Come here with me. Come here, let my love into you."

"I can't do that! I'm not supposed to do that!"

"I've already written to my brother. When he answers we'll take the steamship together. Look what you do to me! Look at it!"

"I want to but—"

"I love you, *Marianuzza*! Take my love inside you!"

That was how she remembered it afterwards, his attenuated voice saying, "Take my love inside you." Those ordinary words carried meaning beyond themselves. Why should she listen to Giuseppina, or the aunt now in America, both of them warning her never to let a man put his "thing" inside her. This was love, this was natural, and Nicolo would be her husband. What did she see in him? The way he carried himself, the way he smiled, knowing he was the only man in her life, that he would take her to a new world where crazy Teresa wouldn't appear every morning clucking like a chicken. Such a small step in her imagination to visualize the old lady laying eggs herself, plucking one from beneath her dress and holding it up between thumb and forefinger! No more crazy Teresa and small-minded people. Nicolo would take her to a place with work and money, and above all he would connect her to life, yes, that fish that no longer frightened her, that monstrous and out-of-proportion thing swollen with desire. She knew how it worked, she knew where that fluid went, and she would open like a flower and it was no longer a monster but something she could tame, something that gave her power.

After that first time she devised ways to do it again. She forgot sheets at the torrent and told Nonna she had to go back. She offered to pick wild fruits and flowers. She volunteered for any task that allowed her out of the house. They met either by the rock or across the stream in a crumbling stone tower, its sides overgrown with vines.

"Kiss me! Kiss me! Tell me you love me!"

"Yes, and now we swim together."

"Promise to take me to L'America! Promise to marry me!"

"Yes, anything you say Marianuzza! Anything you say!"

CHAPTER 8

William drove the cart through a countryside of woods, lakes, and flatlands. Outside of a few poor shacks that belonged to Negroes, Santo saw nothing but sugarcane and cotton plantations with big white houses set far from the road. The plantations were similar, with a stately house for whites, and sheds and shacks for Negroes and animals. The planted fields were cut through with steep banked ditches, whose bare sides suggested both flooding and poor soil. These waterways fed into swamps and long, thin lakes in the midst of the plantings.

If Santo could single out an aspect of L'America to keep him here, it would be this abundance of water. The country seemed nothing but lakes, streams, and ditches, a network of waterways connected like human veins. He thought back to his arrival in New Orleans and how the railroad had followed the Mississippi River. The Sicilians marveled at this vast lake of slow moving water. They were amazed, and spoke of the size and quality of crops this water could produce.

Now he and William passed some Italian crews working in straw hats bought from the camp stores. The figures were blurred by the heat ripples rising from the earth. Santo heard southern Italian voices and he asked William to stop while he listened. Men were singing. He couldn't make out the words, but the choppy yet musical dialect pushed the spirit of these men up into his throat, reminding him to overcome his defeats. The sight of so many Italians hacking away with *zappe* seemed new and terrible and brave. They had no idea where they were and their boss might be cheating them, but they overlooked all this for the sake of work.

Before starting out again William remarked that the work pattern on the plantations was always the same. Italians did the ditching and thinning while Negroes worked the mule-drawn plows and cultivators.

"This is because a mule knows its master's voice and no other," said Santo. "We Sicilians are no strangers to mules."

William smiled at Santo's observation, then turned serious. "Italians work harder with hoes and shovels than Negroes, and everyone knows this. The Italians haven't been discouraged by slavery. They demand more money for their labor, and the whites are willing to pay because without hand labor these plantations are finished. This is why the Italian is the white man's new lover."

Santo watched the cart wheels throw clumps of mud. William's remarks irritated him. The Negro had correctly described himself as a missionary, but what was he preaching? What sins had the Italians committed? They were paid more, but they worked harder. Back home, where the Italians were enslaved by the land managers, they worked for slave wages as the Negroes did here. But Italians were more confident in L'America. They had no history to contend with.

"This country is complicated," Santo said.

"For those who think about it, yes. For those who are selfish and greedy it's like the world everywhere: the strong oppress the weak. That's not complicated."

"You remind me of a man from home," said Santo. "He was an idealist, and saw the world like you. He never spoke of the individual, but of groups."

"Did he tell you to come to L'America?"

"He told me the opposite. He wanted me to stay and organize such men as you see here."

"And what happened?"

"At home we have men as vicious as any. I will come back here, don't worry. I know what to expect now."

"Will you live in the South?"

"I will live anywhere."

William slowed the mule, gave Santo a prolonged look, then urged the animal on. "Be smart and go north. Here the whites still treat the Italians like Negroes and it's a brutality I hope you never experience. Many Sicilians came here to work for the *padroni*. They remained to farm on shares and buy forty-acre plots. But they aren't so happy."

"How can an Italian with land be unhappy?"

William pointed to a turnoff in the road. "We're passing an area where many Sicilians have settled. Your friend Torino owns land there, bought with money stolen from the workers. I'll take you to a man I know, and he'll tell you about life down here."

They came to a small house set on a high bank. Despite a swaybacked roof and a stump foundation, the property was in order. A brick chimney poked through the roof, swabbed with tar at the flashing lines. A small mountain of split firewood was piled by the side door. A mule inside a log pole enclosure worked its rubbery lips on some loose hay. Farther back was a slab-wood shed with a wire pen where piglets and chickens worried a pile of straw and manure. The garden across the road was fenced and trellised for grapes and tomatoes. Rows of raised earth sprouted potatoes, onions, green vegetables, and varieties of squash that Santo had never seen before.

"This man must be rich."

"Compared to Negroes, yes; to Italians, no. To the southern whites he is poor. This place belongs to a Sicilian named Paolo Vaccarella. He knows your old boss, Torino, so be careful what you say, especially to his wife. They're trying to arrange a marriage between Torino and her sister."

Vaccarella was leaning on a porch post. He wore the heavy shoes made by every *calzolaio* in Sicily, thick-soled and high topped. A straw hat was set over his eyes, and hours in the sun had reddened his face. He put a corncob pipe to his lips, and with a practiced motion of his hand, signaled William to run the cart up the bank and behind the house.

William cut the mule with his whip, and as the cart climbed to higher ground Santo recognized Vaccarella's stare, that blankness in which the eyes looked without appearing to see.

Vaccarella met them behind the house. He had mixed gray hair and his eyebrows curled up like wings. When he looked up at Santo the dead stare was gone. His eyes were blue and clear.

"What are you doing with this African? Don't you know these blacks will kill you for a decent pair of Italian shoes?" Smiling, he reached across Santo and took William's hand.

Before Santo could answer, William said, "This one has more to fear from his own kind. Torino almost killed him for trying to leave the camp."

"Torino! Don't you know that he's dead? Killed in New Orleans two days ago!"

"Are you surprised?" asked Santo.

"How can I be surprised? I worked for him once myself, and could kill him just for the food he put in my stomach."

CHAPTER 9

Before Mariana gave herself to Nicolo, she met with her aunt, Angelina, who was about to leave for L'America. The aunt held up her thumb and then turned it down between her open legs. The gesture was explicit.

"Don't let a man put anything in there, ever!"

Mariana had been given that warning along with a second piece of advice that would have avoided her present dilemma. This was the lesson of the white stocking.

Angelina showed Mariana how to stuff a white stocking with clean cotton cloth. This was pinned to her underclothes for the monthly flow.

"How much blood will I lose?" asked Mariana, wondering how all the women she knew had hidden this regular occurrence.

"What you lose will be replaced, especially if you drink a little wine. Only remember, when the blood doesn't come, something is wrong, and until you're married, never let a man put anything in there. Not even his finger! It can start a baby growing. As long as the blood is flowing, there is no danger."

"And how will I know if the blood has stopped for good?"

"Sometimes if you wait, the blood will flow again. But if you are married, none of this matters."

If the aunt had stayed in Sicily to advise Mariana, there would be no problem with the blood. She might have told her what days of the month were safe. Had Mariana known about those days, she would have been more careful. The blood would appear on time, but now the flow had stopped. For three weeks the stocking came away clean.

"Something's in there," she said to Nicolo. She'd gone to the rock with the laundry, but this time she wouldn't stay, not even for kisses.

He reached under the laundry and patted her stomach dismissively. "There's nothing there."

"There is!"

"How do you know?"

"My aunt taught me how to tell."

"Your aunt is in L'America. What does she know?"

"I should be bleeding by now."

"Wait, be patient."

She didn't see him for several days. Then he appeared on the bridge over the laundry pool in a cart loaded with furniture. He caught her eye and looked upstream toward the place where they should meet.

"There's your man," said Giuseppina. "He's packed his goods for somewhere. Who knows? I heard it was Altavilla, but it could be L'America."

"Why is he going to Altavilla?"

"There's a rumor he may get married in Altavilla. He could still keep you after he gets married. Some men will do anything for their appetites. Don't worry, he'll always be hungry that one."

Giuseppina's face ran with sweat, and she spoke with that same sad expression, as if she were about to cry. Her story was well known: her husband had left her with a child and was never heard from again.

"Go to him and be a fool. Everybody knows what you're doing. Most of these women feel sorry for you. Given half a chance, they'd take a knife and dig out his eyes. Go on, ask him about Altavilla."

Mariana gathered up her laundry and splashed toward the bank. She didn't care that the women knew anymore. She had Nicolo's baby in her stomach and they would all be in L'America very soon.

CHAPTER 10

"I'm still not bleeding."

Nicolo was leaning against the rock. At Mariana's words he puffed on his cigar and rolled his eyes as if this meeting was taking too long already. "I told you to wait!"

"My father's coming home."

"Your father." He tapped the ground with one foot impatiently. He took the cigar out of his mouth, studied it, then puffed until the tip glowed. He looked everywhere but at her.

"Will you speak to my father?"

"Your father wants to kill me."

"Why do you say that?"

"On the day he went to L'America he waited for me on the road with a *lupara*." He put both hands together to plead the case that he was the victim.

"You need to speak to him anyway," she said. "This is the way it's done. This is the custom."

"What do you want me to say?" he asked, this time raising his voice.

"You know what."

"No, I don't know!"

"Our marriage, our child."

"There is no child, do you hear me! You have to wait and see if you bleed again."

"How can you say that? What will you say to my father?"

"I'll speak to him." Smoke came out of his mouth in a different direction for each word.

"Swear it!" she said.

"I swear." He patted one hand on his stomach and said, "Are you sure about this? Are you sure about the blood?"

"I'm sure, and I'm afraid."

He'd been leaning against the rock but now he straightened up, ready to leave. He avoided looking her in the eye when he said, "We'll see each other again."

"When?"

"Soon."

"Are you going away?"

"Not really. Don't worry about your father. Don't worry about anything."

"But will we go to L'America?"

"Don't worry about that either!" He crossed the stream and scrambled up the far bank. Once on the road he untied the donkey and climbed into the cart. Without any apparent signal to the animal, man and cart floated away.

She didn't see him for a long time. She decided that if she didn't look, he might appear. She kept away from the balcony and the windows. When Nonna went to morning Mass, Mariana lay on the bed and poked her stomach with her fingers and pressed it with both hands. Maybe it would flatten. Something was in her belly, something more than fear for her father's arrival or the dread of Nicolo's betrayal.

At the laundry pool, Giuseppina said, "You fool. You poor fool. He's gone for good. His family sent him away to be married. Who knows how long it's been arranged."

Her heart dropped into her stomach. Sick with humiliation, she waited for him on the road. She wanted to hear about Altavilla from his lips. She looked into the face of every man returning from the lower valleys. She didn't care who saw her. She waited until darkness spread over the peaks and began to cover the world. Some oil lamps flickered up in the town. When she could no longer make out the men's faces, she started back.

"Get home!"

Something whistled past her ear. A strap cut into her shoulder from behind. It was Nonna with the mule whip, a short stick with a length of harness nailed into the end. The grandmother was skilled with this weapon. The blow to Mariana's head was a deliberate miss, that to the shoulder purposely lightened. Mariana headed for home and Nonna followed, not bothering to conceal the whip.

Mariana sat in the cellar where the hay was banked against a stone wall. She smelled vinegar, olives, preserved tomato—odors possible because her father's mule was gone. The patch of ground in the stall always containing its puddle of stale was now dry and covered with fresh hay as preparation for the homecoming.

She heard Nonna moving around upstairs. The hatchway opened and light penetrated faintly as the old woman came down the ladder. "There's nothing in my hands," she said wearily. "Come up, you have nowhere else to go."

Hot with shame, she twisted a handful of straw around her fingers.

Nonna had come down far enough to bend over and look, first at Mariana, then at the newly prepared stall. "He'll come sooner than you think," she said. "Then only God can protect you. Come, I won't hit you. You're in enough trouble already."

Once upstairs Nonna showed her the letter from L'America.

"When is he coming?"

"Sooner than you think!"

"How do you know?"

"This letter has been read to me. Your father has been to many parts of L'America, even those where the Africans live! He's been to a city called New Orleans, and he'll bring home enough money to take you back with him."

"But when? When will he come?"

"In time for the feast of Peter and Paul."

Alone at the washing pool the next day Mariana soaked and squeezed her father's already clean shirts as preparation for his return. She doubted he'd be home in time for the feast. He was never definite about his coming and going.

She felt an upset in her stomach like a swarm of bees. She had bloody dreams of her father killing Nicolo, then turning her out into the world alone. She had no appetite. She forced herself to eat if only to make Nonna feel better. After eating she would get sick in a bucket. One day the old woman reached out and squeezed her cheeks, studying her face. "I'll make you some tea," she said.

The kitchen faced an open expanse of mountain and valley. This was the lush time of year. The wheat yellowed in tawny swatches. Cloaks of wild grasses encircled the mountain peaks. Yet Mariana saw only desolation and loneliness, a vast and empty scene to which she'd been condemned and a future of shame. How she wanted Nicolo to take her to L'America where they could live near Angelina, who would then laugh with her over this whole adventure. She watched Nonna mix the tea in a pitcher and pour it into bowls. It was medicinal tea, made from strong herbs and chamomile.

"What do you think he'll do to me?"

"One can't tell about your father," she said, pursing her thin lips and blowing noisily across the top of her bowl. "But there's no way to hide your condition."

"Suppose I get married?"

"That rascal won't marry you."

"How do you know?"

"Because he's married already. Everybody knows that."

CHAPTER 11

Santo and Vaccarella watched the cart ease down the bank and lurch over a hump in the road. William looked back and touched his hat: man and cart disappeared into the underbrush.

Vaccarella turned to Santo. "Now tell me what happened with Torino! My wife's sister is coming from home to marry him. Everything has been arranged."

Santo told his story in the chicken house, where it couldn't be overheard by Vaccarella's wife. "I had nothing to do with his death. There were many men in the camp, and we were equally cheated."

"But those who later escaped were well known as troublemakers—all *palermitani*," said Vaccarella as he explored the row of nest boxes, sliding his hand into each one. He calmed the roosting chickens with soft, birdlike whistling. "My wife's taking this very hard, and not only because her sister has lost her chance for a husband. We spoke with those who brought back the body. Torino was carved into pieces, his ears cut off, other parts mutilated. Now, what kind of men would do something like that? There's been enough violence toward Italians already and we must all be careful." He shook his head as he placed some eggs in a bucket.

Santo sat on a barrel and looked through the crudely latticed window at the dense foliage. How could he survive in a place where he had no names for these trees and climbing vines all around him? He was dripping with sweat from this humidity and so far from home. Even Vaccarella, now talking to his chickens as if they were family, was uncertain about life in this place.

"L'America!" said Vaccarella, handing Santo the bucket full of eggs. "This country is rich, but dangerous. Look here!"

He unhooked his overalls and let them fall. One thigh was wrapped in a bandage, and a spot of dried blood showed through. He removed the dressing to expose the wound, a small black hole swabbed over with iodine.

"One shotgun pellet, and the only one to hit me. If you think it was bad for Torino, then look at me. Last week I had to fight about twenty Negroes, a pack of strangers from New Orleans moving north with guns and knives. Lucky for me that I had a good hiding place from which to shoot. I was able to kill one and wound a few more. The law set me free because they don't care what happens to the blacks."

Vaccarella pressed the skin around the wound to check for infection. Santo asked why he hadn't told this story when William was there.

"It wasn't wise to tell him," Vaccarella said. "With blacks the first loyalty is to their own. And why not? Without knowing it, he could pass the information to those who provide food and shelter to these criminals. Listen, if you think there are bandits in Sicily, come to L'America! Here they blow over the land like the wind, and the law is not like ours. Here they arrest a man and then let him go, trusting him to return for his trial. Do you know anything so ridiculous?"

"There's much I don't know about L'America. Is it common for whites and blacks to shoot at each other?"

"It's common for men like this, from the city, to shoot at anything moving. Blacks and whites fear each other everywhere. The whites, especially the Irish in New Orleans, fear the Sicilians because they work so hard. They call us *mafia*, and this is not completely false, but Italians down there have been lynched without trial in case you didn't know. Of course, not so many as for the blacks, who can be killed for looking the wrong way. Italians are in the middle as they rapidly acquire land and build their wealth. This makes them enemies to both sides."

"Torino spoke about such groups of Negroes, but I didn't believe his stories."

"He tells these stories to frighten the Sicilians because he thinks they've seen nothing of the world. This is the way these *padroni* work." Vaccarella waved a hand as if there was a bothersome insect between them. Then he touched Santo's shoulder. "Come into my house and let the dead go their way."

He led Santo into a room with an igloo-shaped oven in the middle. Several round loaves of bread lay on the nearby brickwork. Holy statues, votive candles, and other religious items were arranged on a shelf along one wall. Against another wall was a wood-burning stove. Pots were steaming and Santo took in the smells of beans and boiling tomatoes. The aroma weakened his knees and he could have kissed the split-log floor had it not been for his next sight: a dark, frowning boy in a corner of the room with a double barreled shotgun pointed at his feet. The hammers were pulled back.

Vaccarella's son was muscular, barefoot, and shirtless. His nipples were the color of clay and he wore heavy pants drawn tight with rope. His black hair grew in all directions. At a signal from his father he released the hammers and raised the shotgun. Then he went outside without saying a word.

"I'm sorry for this," said Vaccarella, "but the recent trouble makes it necessary. The boy trusts nobody. This house and the acres of land were once rented to blacks. But the landowners would rather sell land to Sicilians. They call us "dagos," but we're willing to pay more money, and always in cash. We know the meaning of interest! But sometimes the blacks try to take their old places back, claiming them as their homes. What can we do?" He clapped his hands twice and cried, "Vincenzina!"

A short, stout woman came through the door the son had been guarding. One arm hugged a large bowl in which she was beating eggs. She set down the bowl, keeping her eyes fixed on Santo. A folded newspaper appeared from under her apron. She showed him the headline: DAGO BOSS BUTCHERED.

"What do you know about this?" she asked.

"Stay calm now," said Vaccarella, approaching the table on which dinner had been arranged. "He told me everything."

"This has been translated by our priest," she said, tapping the headline with her finger. "Torino was found near the waterfront in New Orleans. They cut off his ears and fingers and other things as well! Now several men are missing from the camp, including yourself!"

"Sit down and eat," said Vaccarella, putting a hand on Santo's shoulder and holding the other out to restrain his wife. "He's explained everything. And who nearly beat him to death at that camp? Our future brother-in-law! And why? You know why! Besides that, why would this man here appear in our part of the country if Torino was killed in New Orleans?"

"Perhaps he arranged it."

"I told you what happened!" cried Vaccarella, raising his voice so loud that the son looked in at the door. Vaccarella motioned him away. "Come, Regina, eat! She's worried about her sister, not the man who's dead."

"She's coming from home to marry him, and now what?" Vincenzina's breath came quickly, and under her dress, made tight by the apron, her breasts heaved. She picked up the bowl of eggs and wiped her eyes with the back of one hand.

"Don't cry into the eggs," said Vaccarella. His appeal broke her mood, and she started beating the eggs again, still studying Santo. Vaccarella said, "This man here spoke out. He told the other men they were being cheated."

Vincenzina held her stare at Santo. She had dark crescents under her eyes. She stopped beating the eggs. "Why did you make trouble?"

Santo pushed his plate forward, aware of Vaccarella's gestures for him to be silent and eat. He said, "Listen to me. I'm a widower with two children. The day is gone when I can take chances. I did some things in the camp, yes. I read the book in which Torino falsely recorded the purchase of things never bought. When he discovered that I'd helped the men, he threatened me. When I tried to leave the camp I was beaten, and my money stolen—thirty dollars American sent by a sister in New York who works for her money like the rest of us. Do I accuse Torino of taking my money? Yes, even though it could have been the blacks. But believe me, I had nothing to do with his death. If you don't wish to believe what I say, perhaps it's better I leave this house. I understand we're near a railroad station."

Vincenzina slid the newspaper back under her apron and began beating the eggs again. She motioned her husband to keep Santo's plate full, then she looked away, taking the first step in a thinking process. "So the world turns," she said. "But I didn't know you were a family man. Where are you going now, back to Castellano? You have somebody there, I'm sure. Those towns are full of women now." She winked at Vaccarella. She'd been speaking in dialect to signal that formalities with Santo were over.

How well Santo knew these Sicilian women. They changed their emotions like clothes, getting their men to do whatever they wanted. The women in Castellano had the same aggressive quality, and tried to put him at a disadvantage because he was a widower with children.

He looked up at Vaccarella, who put one finger under his eye to show that his wife was crafty.

"This is why she wants to go to New York. She wants to open a *grosseria*, but she really wants to find a husband for her sister, who won't live in this country alone. But why should we give up this farm?"

"We can sell it!" she cried. "New York is the place to make money. It's full of Italians. Look at Regina's sister."

Vaccarella sat back. "She slowly convinces me, a little every day. There's nothing for us here, a decent life but little money, and all this trouble with blacks. The whites want us to push them out, and meanwhile the whites treat us like them." He drew his index finger across his neck. "It always comes down to property. That was why we left Sicily."

Vincenzina turned to Santo. "Do you have a woman back home? If not you should meet my sister in New York when we move there."

"Why do you make this offer when you hardly know me?"

"We know you well enough, and you need a wife, that's clear. In L'America one must take advantage. Perhaps you've come to our house as God's gift for a woman whose marriage wasn't meant to be. To tell you the truth, they weren't suitable. Torino had money, that's all. What do you say, Regina, you can meet my sister. Her name is Rafaella and believe me, she's a different type, not afraid of a man with children."

After dinner Santo walked alone in the orchard. Vaccarella had given him a Toscano, and Santo found a dry place and sat with his back against a fruit tree. He lit the cigar and relaxed now that he was with people he could trust. Night came on and he blew smoke playfully at the moon. His head and his ribs still ached from the beating he'd taken. There was no way to know what was happening at home, but he was lucky to be alive, to be filled with food, lucky that someday, perhaps, he'd meet Vacarella's sister-in-law. That brazen Vincenzina was right about L'America: one had to act fast.

CHAPTER 12

The drumming began on the eve of the feast of Castellano's patron saints. Nonna tacked a cloth over the pantry window and cleared a space for Mariana to pray. For two hours in the morning and two more in the afternoon she was to pray for her father's safe return. She was to pray for the steamship and its captain. She was to pray against theft and storms and all evils befalling travelers.

"Let him find you with the rosary in your hand," she said. "Pray to Saints Peter and Paul."

Mariana listened to the drumbeats calling the two saints. Her ability to pray and believe had its limits. She didn't believe that Peter and Paul could save her from the baby inside her or even from the hot wind of love. She still had that. She imagined their passage to L'America on a steamship crossing the wide ocean—how she would comfort him during the voyage! They would take refuge with his brother and Angelina, who would become their allies, providing work, a place to live, arranging for an Italian priest to perform the marriage. Relatives and new friends would protect her against the angry parents on both sides.

The drumming came closer, each beat harsh and explosive. She pulled the window cloth aside and saw a small boy with a drum on his back. The drum was bigger than the boy. Behind him walked the drummer, an old man named Calogero who looked angrily at the Regina house, then struck a hard blow.

She went to the feast with Nonna the next night. Walking with locked arms, they passed Teresa, who'd set up a table outside her door for selling eggs. After an exchange of greetings the old woman said, "And where is the man of your house? Mother of God, what he'll find when he returns!" She winked at Mariana, then made a motion with her hand to signify punishment.

The grandmother pushed Mariana along. "Come, be strong. Tonight you'll see the saints. Maybe they can tell you something."

They stood on the uphill side of the piazza as the procession began. Cologero and the drum bearer took the lead, followed by small children carrying paper lanterns. Then came a file of older boys with burning wheat sheaves. The saints emerged from the church, borne by men and older boys and teetering on platforms strewn with flowers, coins, photographs, and lira notes of small denomination.

Nonna grasped Mariana's elbow to get her attention. "Look how beautiful!" She clasped her hands fervently. "There's nothing like the church to show us what's pure, to show us how to live. Look! Here's Saint Cecelia wearing the Crown of Martyrs. She was blind, you know, and gave her life for Jesus Christ. And there's Saint Lucy, who appears to be sleeping. But see her eyes on the plate she carries? She tore them out to drive away her lover. Remember, my dear, Jesus will forgive any sin! Jesus will never reject you."

Mariana pulled Nonna close. She wished it were true about Jesus. The old woman felt warm in the cool night. Mariana loved her for trying to help, but Nonna couldn't stand up to her father. He would swoop onto the house like a hawk. The old woman would be silent before him.

"Any sin," repeated the grandmother. "He will forgive any sin."

Mariana scanned the crowded piazza. Banks of candles burned in the church portico. People joined in the procession. Boys fed their burning sheaf ends into a bonfire. Mariana reminded herself that every soul in this piazza harbored sin. But how could she confess what she'd done? She would have to describe it to a priest, who might ask for details. Would the priest ask about the "fish?" Would he want to know exactly what she'd been thinking? How could she explain that she'd gambled her soul for love. Despite the presence of all these holy saints, her body was still hot with desire. When she and Nicolo were together she didn't care if her soul burned in eternal fire.

People eating pumpkin seeds and roasted chickpeas passed before the bonfire flames as Mariana tried to read the sins on their faces. Thievery, lust, betrayal, adultery, she wasn't the only one. Pairs of accusing eyes rolled in her direction and held fast when she stared back. But was her soul the blackest? Other eyes read her like a book, but she read their eyes too. She drew in the night air and gripped Nonna tightly. The old woman gave her strength.

More statues emerged from the church, and the crowd cheered each saint as it came into the open. The last to join the procession was a statue of Jesus, an outsized rosary wrapped around his hand. From where she stood, Mariana could recognize one of the bearers—Nicolo.

CHAPTER 13

On the first laundry day after the feast she met him at the rock. He was leaning back with his eyes half closed, an unlit cigar dangling from his lips. He looked different. He'd exchanged his cap for a hat with a brim, and the donkey had been replaced by a young mule with a copper-colored nose. It was tied nearby and preferred to look at them rather than crop grass.

"So your new wife gave you the hat and that well-fed animal. What else did she give you?"

"Nothing."

"And what did I give you?"

"Everything."

"And what did you do about it?"

"Nothing."

"Then what are you doing back here?" she asked, stiffening and holding her ground when he tried to pull her close. She smelled the stable, tobacco, wine. She smelled wealth.

"I came back for you," he said.

"And your wife?"

"A mistake."

"So soon?"

Her words seemed to wake him up. He looked around quickly and tried to undo the buttons of her dress. She slapped his hands away.

"Where is your father?" he asked.

"He's coming any day now."

"But he's not here yet. Meet me tomorrow."

"For what?"

"I know when the steamships arrive from L'America. There are none now, and none expected for at least one week. Your father won't be home until then. You can still meet me here tomorrow. Your grandmother thinks I'm gone and she'll never suspect. My marriage means nothing. My wife means nothing."

"And what do I mean?"

"Everything."

She met him the next day and once again didn't allow him to touch her, at least at first. He promised never to abandon her and she desperately wanted to believe him.

"If you can abandon your wife, how do I know you won't abandon me?"

He answered with declarations of love; and while in the past these words were only spoken when he made love, or was aroused to love, his words now gave her hope that he truly loved her. He was testing to see if she was strong enough to bear with him. She tried not to give in, but moved by his words she let him turn her against the rock and he pressed her hard, kissing her between neck and shoulder, raking her desperately with his teeth. She clamped her legs so he couldn't enter. She bit her lip to avoid crying out and alerting the other women. He tore at her top and pulled it down. He squeezed her breasts as if to milk them. She saw him as a beast, like some brute from a fairy tale with fangs, wings, claws. Why did he want her so violently?

"I'm angry with myself because I left you," he said.

She turned around and they kissed with open mouths as if to eat each other, as if she had also become a beast. The black curls under his new hat glistened with sweat. Through her tear-filmed eyes she watched his teeth dig into her shoulder and rake her down. She knew that no other woman could put him in such a state, and during their lovemaking she forced him to admit this truth over and over.

CHAPTER 14

Upon arriving in New Orleans, Santo walked through the French Quarter, stunned to find the streets full of Sicilian vendors speaking his dialect. Many stores were Sicilian owned. He found Don Vito in a storefront bank on Barracks Street. The long, monk-like beard he'd worn in Sicily was now a well-trimmed goatee. He recognized Santo at once, and the two men sat down.

Santo leaned forward and put both hands on the table, palms down. He looked at two cups of coffee, then into Don Vito's face. It was a new face, but the same man.

Santo said slowly, "Did you know that I was nearly killed for your ideas, once here and once at home?"

Don Vito cocked his head and smiled. "Those were other men's ideas, anarchism and the like. Once in the air they fly like seeds." He fluttered the fingers of one hand as if his former self had flown away.

Santo looked around the room and saw money everywhere—men were spending it, men were saving it. Owned by enterprising Italians, these banks provided services such as money exchange and transfer to Italy, job finding, letter writing, legal work, travel arrangements, even shaving and haircutting, done in a back room where Santo saw a pair of occupied barber chairs. The world was moving ahead without him.

Don Vito had replaced the dreary peasant clothing worn in Castellano with a silver tie and a stiff-collared shirt. He was buttoned into a striped suit with sharply pleated trousers. A gold chain hung between his vest pockets.

Santo gestured around the room and said, "So this is what you do now?"

Don Vito's expression went blank, as if the question had offended him. Then he smiled once again. "With each moment, Regina, my memory intensifies. That day in Castellano when we met is clear to me now. As soon as I saw you in the crowd I said to myself, "Here is the man who can serve me."

He reached across the table and patted Santo's hand. And then with a slight flourish he waved his index finger in a circle to indicate that Santo should look around the room. In addition to the men depositing money at the teller's cage, a group had gathered at the work agency desk. Most of them had chalk marks on their hats and jackets to indicate recent entry into the country. Don Vito explained that these men would leave at once to pick fruit on farms north of the city. These jobs were arranged for a fee, which was paid to the bank owner.

"Look around you, Regina, and you'll see an organization whose purpose is to serve the Italian, not rape him. Let's say I'm in another part of the same business."

Don Vito took Santo's hand and pulled it gently to get his attention. "Listen to me. I know the plantation where you worked. I know the one called Zillo, too, and he's on his way back home, thanks to me. All the bankers in the Italian quarter know of Torino. Death was his fortune, and the Irish police don't care. Torino was just one more dago." Don Vito raised one hand and moved it in a small circle to signify death. "Zillo told me what you did in the work camp. The fact that you haven't mentioned his name in order to gain my favor speaks well. You've proved yourself to me. Now, tell me, what can I do for you?"

Santo sat down on the edge of the chair. For some reason he wanted to get up and leave. He looked away while Don Vito beckoned him to speak. There was a steady traffic in and out of the bank. Everyone was shaping a life. He remembered Vincenzina's words: In L'America one must take advantage.

"Come," said Don Vito. "What will you have?"

"A job until the next steamship. That's all I ask."

"Jobs are more plentiful than ideas," said Don Vito.

He then arranged a job as an iceman's helper, and Santo rode the streets of New Orleans in a two-horse cart. He lugged blocks of ice into saloons and restaurants. He slept in a home filled with as many men as could squeeze into rooms with floor-to-ceiling bunks. All the men were transient, remaining briefly before moving out to the plantations and fruit farms. These were contract labor jobs with pay as high as two dollars a day, but with a commitment of two months or more. Santo didn't have that kind of time. He had to get home. He had to check on his family.

Every so often he added an American dollar to a thin folding of bills hidden in his jacket lining. He took his meals at the boarding house, then walked along the wharf. When thoughts of home and family made him maudlin and sleepless, he drank in one of the wine shops operated from private homes. Here he met Italians from every part of the old country, stonecutters from the north, thieves and opportunists from the south, surly and devious types from Palermo and Catania, and peasants from everywhere, *contadini* who'd worked for middlemen from Sicily to Switzerland.

The boarding house overlooked a muddy creek which cut through an open space occupied by a garden and a shed filled with firewood and roosting chickens. A pack of inbred cats lived under the back porch. There were more cats than Santo could count, and when the door opened they roiled up from below and milled about for something to eat. The cats were dwarfed and deformed, commonly missing tails, ears, and sometimes legs. Some were blind; when scraps were thrown on the walkway, they ran the wrong way and lapped at mud until they realized it wasn't food. Santo watched the deformed and desperate cats with the feeling that he was like them, unfit for the world and scurrying to the wrong place for money. He had a life to build and a daughter to protect and there were moments when he felt completely inadequate. That was his unchanging thought. There was no such thing as the freedom to go where he pleased, to make friends with these other Italians and travel with them to Texas to pick fruit, or even to California, where a wine industry was developing.

At night he pulled the thread from his jacket lining and folded another dollar inside. Then he sat on the porch with a cigar, blowing smoke at the mosquitoes and watching the cats scramble for the dinner slops thrown by his landlord, who kept the cats because they killed every rat in sight. When the poor creatures returned to their places under the walkway, he would watch the sun set over some low wooden buildings. The Negroes would be returning from work on foot, and Santo would think about the sickening food the old woman had given him in the slave house, and how all creatures, not only the cats so desperate for food but human beings as well, learned to live in their particular place and became one with it, and how the Italian peasant was as much a product of his soil as cats or plants or Negroes or any organism supported by what the earth produced. The wrinkled, sere and organic men plying the Sicilian roads lived on wheat and beans and greens and oil and wine and fruit. They consumed these as their animals consumed the wheat chaff and the bean pods and the grass and the weeds. They had an existence no different from growing matter. The poor man didn't have the luxury of thought, as did the upper classes like Don Vito, who could throw ideas into the wind like chaff. Don Vito could afford to entertain himself with his own thoughts, but peasants were one with the soil, organic matter coming from it, looking like it, and they would eventually return to it and fertilize it.

His wife had been a living example of that. She was a small, dark woman, as rugged as a mule. When he first saw her she was throwing grain to chickens with quick efficient motions of her arm, and from this she immediately went to her next task, which was to spread laundry over bushes to dry. Her long hair was bunched up and tied with a red-flowered kerchief, and she wore a handmade shawl over her shoulders as bright as the bluest sky. She died like a plant cut down by a sickle. Neither doctor nor midwife nor witch nor the oldest hag in Castellano could explain how one minute found her shelling peas and the next on her back gasping with a fearful noise from somewhere deeper than the center of her being, like the death throes of some mythic beast. Even in death she seemed larger than life.

CHAPTER 15

On departure day Santo waited to board the *Florida* when someone gripped his elbow from behind and pulled him back. Turning abruptly, he looked down on a short man wearing a straw hat with an unsnapped brim under which an angry look had been fixed. The man's face was puffy and scarred, and after scrutinizing Santo for a long moment he said, "Let me see your documents."

"Who are you?"

"The police." He displayed a badge inside a billfold and taking Santo roughly by the arm, pulled him further from the steerage line and held him while he examined the ticket and passport.

"The man I want is your size, and even looks like you. He is guilty of the most audacious criminal and civil delicts. But he is older, and speaks with a *palermitano* accent. Yours has a hint of the countryside. Where are you from?"

"You wouldn't know it," said Santo.

"But tell me anyway."

"Castellano del Torre."

"He has been there."

"Who?"

"The man I seek." He tipped his hat. "I am Giuseppe Petrosino, a police inspector from New York City." He turned back into the crowd without another word. He carried an umbrella, and after leaving Santo he continued along the dock, using the umbrella as a cane and peering into the faces of taller men.

Santo was soon stopped by a man he recognized from the bank.

"Cousin! What are you doing in New Orleans?" He slapped Santo's back with a newspaper and pressured him to move forward. Then he whispered, "Don Vito wants to see you. Don't worry, you'll return in time for departure."

They took a fast carriage to the ice factory where Santo had worked. Don Vito sat in the office dressed in a shabby black suit and a slouch hat. A long-stemmed pipe hung from one side of his mouth. The messenger left the room and the two men drew up wooden crates. Don Vito lit the pipe and slowly blew out a puff of smoke.

"You were called because I too am sailing on the *Florida*. But there are some who would prevent my leaving." He took the pipe from his mouth and pointed the stem at Santo. "You know there was political trouble at home. Some of the organizers were killed by the *carabinieri*, who blamed innocent people for their murders. These accusations have followed me to the other side of the ocean."

"Then why do you go home?"

"It will be easier to hide there."

"So you are wanted by the American police?"

Don Vito nodded.

"Is one of them a short man with a straw hat?"

Don Vito turned pale at first, then his blood rose in irregular patches. "How do you know this man?"

Santo described the meeting on the pier with Petrosino. Don Vito stood up and paced the room, rubbing his chin. Then he sat down, so close to Santo this time that their knees almost touched. He looked up with that open, direct expression, as if Santo were the only other person in the world.

"This is why I asked you here. When a steamship sails it's easy for the local police to capture anyone they want. But my looks are known to this fat little worm, as your meeting with him proves."

Don Vito drew the pipe to life, then took it from his mouth and used it to gesture.

"Understand this, of you I ask nothing, demand nothing. What is between us will be done as friends. I can elude this wretched Neapolitan, but it would delay my trip, and I'm as eager as you to return home. The question is whether our friendship will build."

Later in the day, and from the first-class level of the ship, Santo looked down at the crowded dock where Petrosino was trying to find Don Vito among the first- and second-class passengers. Don Vito's plan had been simple but effective. He and Santo had exchanged tickets, Don Vito taking Santo's steerage pass, and Santo taking the Don's first-class ticket, issued to someone named Salvatore Gemelli. Since the steamship officials never questioned first and second class passengers, his processing had been rapid.

Santo watched Petrosino, positioned between the first- and second-class gangplanks, looking from one to the other like a spectator at a tennis match. At the same time, farther down the pier, on the steerage gangway, Don Vito was boarding the ship with the file of Italian returnees, a stuffed pillowcase on his shoulder to hide his face.

A short time later and on board the ship, a hand rested on Santo's shoulder, and Don Vito gently pulled him back from the railing. They proceeded to the steerage level, this trip facilitated by a crewman deferential to Don Vito. And now, from the steerage railing, one level closer to the pier, they could see Petrosino still watching the gangplanks.

"What do you know about that man?" asked Santo.

"He's the kind that only L'America would create, for back home he would dry up like a pellet of goat shit. Here he grows like a garden snail, never any longer, but always fatter. He was hired by the Americans to combat the "Italian Criminal," of which he finds one at the end of every shovel. Many innocent people have been deported by this man." Don Vito had no sooner finished speaking when Petrosino, with some ship's officials, came up the steerage gangplank.

"Perhaps he'll arrest both of us."

"He cannot. This ship is Italian property. It would be the same as an American policeman trying to arrest a man in Italy without the government's permission. He can come on board only as a visitor."

No sooner had Don Vito spoken these words than farther down the deck a steel door flew open with a jarring squeak of hinges. Petrosino came along briskly, loudly tapping his umbrella tip on the deck. His eyes were fixed straight ahead, as if he hadn't noticed either Santo or Don Vito. Only when he walked past them did he stop and turn, as if his initial oversight had been a trick. He spun around, pointed his umbrella at Don Vito, and said, "You were lucky this time." He pulled out a folded piece of legal paper and waved it. "Come back to this country and I'll be happy to serve you."

"Maybe it's your turn to be my guest, in Sicily," replied Don Vito.

"I'll do that," said the detective. "I'll do that sooner than you think."

With a long look at Santo, Petrosino continued on his way.

"It's too bad he saw me," said Don Vito as the ship pulled away from the harbor with Petrosino still watching them. "And now he knows you, too, and for this I must apologize and someday repay you. I'll tell you now, this man never forgets a face."

Santo didn't believe that a detective would come all the way to New Orleans from New York to find Don Vito because of political trouble back home. And he soon discovered another reason for Petrosino's visit. After settling into the steerage compartment he had a chance to read old copies of Italian- language newspapers that some passengers had brought along. Most of these newspapers were published in New York City, and one story from a few years back had the following headline:

WOMAN FINDS DEAD BODY PACKED IN SAWDUST BARREL. MORELLO GANG ARRESTED—OTHER MEN SOUGHT BY DETECTIVE PETROSINO

The story named Vito Cascio Ferro as the leader of a gang notorious in New York City for murder and extortion. Santo puzzled over the way Don Vito could move so easily from politics to crime. In this account of the barrel murder, the man's genitals had been cut off and stuffed into his mouth, a Black Hand punishment for violating the code of silence. These were the habits of home. This was why men like Simone were treading the mountain roads with clay jugs bouncing on the backs of their goats, their eyes looking straight ahead. When the *Florida* docked in Palermo, Santo would politely take leave of Don Vito, fetch his mule, and ride back to Castellano, where there could be trouble enough. Then he might wish for the quality that would enable him to pack a dead man in sawdust.

One day Don Vito came down to the steerage deck and spoke to him. "My friend, since the moment we met in New Orleans, I saw you were preoccupied. You didn't need to tell me that you wanted more out of life than these others. Now, listen to me. In New Orleans I spoke with those who worked with you at the plantation. They aren't the kind of men I like to have around me: they're hotheads, and we know what crimes they can commit."

Santo had been looking through the rail at the tilting, luminous ocean, well aware of Don Vito's serious demeanor. This man didn't relate his actions to everyday survival, but to the world. This was why, when everyday needs came to him he paid no attention to them. This was the way to live, and it was a gift. If Don Vito had a daughter about to be compromised, he would hypnotize her into virtue, and the lover into obsequious fear. Yet Santo could not, in the widest stretch of his imagination, see Don Vito's hands in a barrel of sawdust, or conceive of him extorting hard-earned dollars in the Italian quarters of any city. Looking up, he said, "I've read of this Petrosino in the newspapers and so I can't pretend to know nothing."

The remark seemed to sail past Don Vito on the breeze, for he moved his head as if watching it go by. "You're an intelligent man, and I know you'll understand what I'm about to say. I've traveled in many parts of the world, and it's the same everywhere. There are men who take power, and men who surrender it. This is the way of things, and it has nothing to do with whether a man is good or bad. When a man follows his natural way, there is no fear. The necessary power will come to him. But this isn't so with our friend, the detective, who is a hunting dog without a nose."

"What would he have done to you?"

"He would have taken me to New York, where in the privacy of his office he would have beaten me until my teeth fell out, or I lost my hearing or part of my sight, as was the case with others falling into his hands. And then having no evidence to charge me with a crime, he would have taken my money and thrown me into the street. You prevented this, my friend."

"But surely there were other men who could have served you just as well."

Don Vito laughed. "But none as tall as you, or with the same abilities. You may think I'm joking, or trying to compliment you unfairly. But you're not like these others. Had I asked some poor peasant for this favor he would have gone to pieces with one look from that miserable policeman." Don Vito rocked back and forth, looking dreamily at the ocean. "Will you return to L'America?"

"This depends on what I find at home."

"Trouble?"

"Perhaps."

"What kind of trouble?"

Santo shook his head and Don Vito nodded sympathetically. He continued to look out over the ocean. "I see you're a man who dislikes favors, so I offer none. Many men suspect favors. These are men truthful to the hilt, real Sicilians, creatures of loyalty—which is the father of truth. I'll say no more. I'm well known in the town of Bisacquino. Look for me there if you need help."

CHAPTER 16

Santo concealed himself in the trees upstream from the laundry pool and listened to the women's voices. He was tired and shaking, still part of the shuddering steamship where the power of revolving steel had pushed against the ocean. He'd been in the world, but now he was back to isolation, to the chirping of birds, the smell of rosemary, the saw of crickets. He was back inside that giant bubble of thin air in which these expressions of life were a tiny and absurd testament to existence. He'd returned to those lives that would have more meaning if they packed up and left, allowing their houses to melt back into the stones.

He could never again live with this uneventful silence. His visit to L'America had given the lie to Don Vito's advice that he should stay here and fight for justice. One year ago the *Fasci* marched triumphantly into Castellano proclaiming a new era. Now the movement was dormant, many of its members escaped overseas, the leaders dead or disappeared. Those tenacious enough to believe in the cause would follow their fortune to death, jail, or lifelong poverty. Those who knew how to ride the movement, and when to quit, like Don Vito, would reap new rewards. But the meek would remain behind to inherit nothing. What wind would carry Santo? This depended on the sixteen-year-old about to come up from the laundry pool. She was pregnant and the whole town knew it.

Now the women approached, some with bundled laundry on their heads. This was an assortment of women, some heavy, some tiny and wiry, some shy, some huffing and complaining, some with all the beauty of youth, women he could have married, and whose skilled fingers gripping clean garments gave him a surge of desire. He longed to end this widower's life in which his desire for women was overshadowed by a concern for his children and the need to make a living.

The file of women topped the bank and went their separate ways. They were now partly hidden by the thick honeysuckle and grotesque cactus plants that grew from the spaces in the retaining wall along the road. Santo moved closer to the path, and not seeing Mariana, headed down to the pool. He held the pistol in his pocket with the hammer down. At the pool he concealed himself. Mariana was washing clothes, alone in the middle of the stream.

For a few moments he imagined a salving effect on his anger in the indifferent rush of the water, and his daughter's practiced motions, those rhythms of hand and body common to his people. What he was soon to confirm might push him to the brink of something he hoped life would spare him—a specific trouble that would define his life: Santo Regina, the widower whose daughter was pregnant, had killed a man. And his new life in L'America—held out by a letter from Vincenzina Vaccarella, that her sister would now be pleased to meet him in New York—might never be possible.

Mariana came toward him along the stream bank. She carried the bunched-up laundry in front to hide her condition. She labored with her weight as Santo stepped onto the path. She was several steps away before noticing him. She paused to draw breath, then came up slowly and stopped, leaning over the laundry to kiss him. He turned away from her kiss and wrenched the laundry from her hands. Here was a show for all the town.

He struck her on the side of the face with his open hand. "Where is that ugly beast?"

"I don't know."

"I'll tell you then. He lives in Altavilla, with his wife. Are you surprised that he used you for what he wanted?"

"He promised to marry me. He said we would go to L'America. He promised to talk to you."

"And you believed him." Santo looked around to see if anyone was witnessing this display of shame and stupidity. He raised his hand again. Now he could beat her until her eyes bled.

She covered her face, crying soundlessly, her body shaking.

He lowered the raised hand to her shoulder. "You love him and he's married to someone else? What does this tell you?"

"His parents forced him to marry! He told me!"

"Go home."

While Mariana continued on, Santo followed the path back to

the rock where she and Nicolo had been meeting. He walked among desiccated piles of manure and patches of cropped grass, evidence of Nicolo's presence like a slap in the face. He crossed the stream and followed a footpath to a stone tower on the opposite bank, a tower older than time. He climbed a stone stairway to the top. Now he stood above the bridge that spanned the pool. The quilted countryside stretched down and away, then up again on the far mountains. The sheep and cattle grazing in the lower valleys looked like children's toys. All was quiet as he looked for Nicolo on the road below.

Enveloped in a heavy, floral smell, he heard the flicker of birds and the distant rush of water. He wasn't sure what he would do if he saw Nicolo. It wasn't a simple matter of putting an end to a young man's life, of violating this momentarily blessed silence with the firing of a weapon. His solution to this problem would come out of his past. It would come from his character, and there was a childhood incident by which he defined himself, and while waiting for Nicolo to come along, he thought about it.

There'd been a Castellanese named Vincenzo who'd spent his life on a fishing boat out of Trapani and had come home to retire. He was an old man burnt by the sun with lined, leathery skin, and every day he sat with the other old men in the piazza. Vincenzo was a man of regularity. He arrived at the same time every evening, smoked the same number of cigarettes, and carried a raw egg in his jacket pocket. At exactly five o'clock by the church bell he poked a hole in each end of the egg with the point of a knife and sucked it dry with a quick motion of egg to mouth. Then he returned the shell to his pocket.

One day he didn't eat the egg, but none of the other men seemed to notice. As the light faded the men started for home, walking with the unsteadiness of old age down the narrow streets that fell off from the piazza.

The next morning Vincenzo was still there, eyes and mouth open, as if amazed that the next breath hadn't come. Men said later that Gangiuseppe, a local monk unfairly denied sainthood, had been seen on the evening of the old man's death. The monk was said to walk the streets of Castellano when all were sleeping. He was chiefly noted for his visits to those about to die. Any witness pure of soul would be able to see him with the hood of his cowl removed if the deceased were going to heaven; but if the object of the monk's visit was going to hell, the hood would cover his face

It was said that the last man to leave the piazza that night walked past the reposed Vincenzo and caught a glimpse of Gangiuseppe's homespun fluttering near the old man's body. This witness may have heard the monk's famous exhortation uttered near the person about to die: "O what an odor of Paradise!" The witness hadn't seen whether the monk's hood was up or down, thus it was never decided whether Vincenzo had gone to heaven or hell.

The witness was Santo's father, Franco, a man with a bitter sense of humor. He was the only man in the piazza who didn't habitually dress like a mourner, preferring a well-washed gray jacket with matching cap, and a shirt with fine blue stripes. Franco was a good Catholic, but because of his dislike of the local priest he never attended Mass.

When Franco revealed that he'd seen and heard the monk, many Castellanese, led by the town's zealous priest, questioned him at great length. The priest believed the monk could still be sanctified. Everyone wanted to know the exact circumstances of the event: where Franco was standing, what time of evening, whether he'd taken any wine or influential herbs at his midday meal, and last of all, whether the monk's hood was up or down.

"Didn't you look up?" asked the priest, whose name was Giovanni. He'd come with pen and paper to interview Franco in the piazza. "Surely you looked into the distant hills where there's light. Surely outlined against this light you must have seen whether his head was bare!"

Franco wouldn't answer. Father Giovanni was the least likely man to extract a story from him anyway. Franco nursed an old grudge against the priest, who'd cut short his career as an altar boy, driving him into bitterness and the abandonment of his boyhood dream to become a Jesuit missionary.

It happened this way: One Sunday morning before serving at Mass, Franco had eaten a half-liter of fresh ricotta donated to the rectory. The sweet cheese was a treat but it produced an urgent need for a bowel movement soon after the Mass got under way. This need became more pressing as the mass continued, with Franco squirming to relieve his discomfort.

Father Giovanni considered this demeanor during the Mass as a sacrilegious distraction, but his angry looks discouraged Franco from abandoning the altar. Disheartened that the priest didn't appreciate his dilemma, the boy lost control, surrendering to the pressure of the burning liquid, which ran down his thighs and stuck to his cassock. When he rose from a kneeling position, he saw that his shoes were soiled. The odor struck the priest as he was preparing the chalice for consecration of the Host.

Father Giovanni stopped the Mass and ushered Franco out, making repeated signs of the cross to save face before the congregation. Once in the rectory he struck the boy with such a flurry of blows that the smacks were heard in the church. This embarrassment caused Franco to lose control of his bowels once again, which drove the priest to greater insults and violence.

Franco neither served nor attended Mass after that. He forswore his oath to become a missionary. He refused to acknowledge Father Giovanni in public, and when he was older and strong enough to look at the man directly, he stared with such an arrogance that the priest avoided him. By then Franco no longer set foot in any church.

Some Castellanese thought that by promoting the holy monk to sainthood, the priest was trying to further his own ends. They reasoned that Franco had actually seen one of the town's numerous rats, drawn by the smell of Vincenzo's body. Others believed the rat may have been attracted by the egg in Vincenzo's pocket.

Santo saw that his father enjoyed the sense of power his testimony gave him. His father never changed the basic story, but would color it one way or the other, either to keep the argument going or to aggravate the priest, who often took part in the discussions.

His father would say, "Yes, I saw something the color of a chestnut. Of course, it could have been anything. But there was a flow to it, a definite flow, and perhaps a holy aspect."

"But you heard the voice! You heard the holy monk's words! You said so!"

"The words, of course. I heard words, but I didn't see the monk."

One of the cynics then said to the priest, "Excuse me for being indelicate, Father, but we must be free to speak in such matters. The dead man was already beginning to smell. His body was obviously releasing gas. Perhaps this is what the good man heard."

"Did you hear the voice or not?" asked the priest.

"I've already said what I heard."

The event was discussed for years, and Santo came to realize that Gangiuseppe's appearance was the only event to transport these men beyond their slumbering bitterness, the only instance when his father could display his distance from the monotonous life around him.

His mother said that idleness caused men to waste themselves. "Your father shares the vices of the idle," she said. "He thinks he's better than the others."

Santo learned much later that his father's vision had been more incredible than he cared to reveal. Franco had seen Gangiuseppe, but not at the base of the statue. When he awoke from his sleep and started home, passing the sleeping fisherman, he looked into the purple, hazy distance and saw the monk hovering in vaporous space, suspended just above eye level, as distinct in detail as the statue of Gangiuseppe carried on feast day. For a split second Franco thought it was the actual statue in defiance of gravity since the monk's habit hung as if the statue from the nearby church had floated into the air. But then he saw that the monk's face was human, with that cadaverous texture created by the suffocating rectory. The monk floated in a vague, steamy mist, emitting a noise like a hummingbird or giant wasp, a suspiration, as if wings were beating; and embedded in that noise, in which the monk's lips moved in rough approximation, was the prophetic utterance, "O what an odor of Paradise!" like a voice from underwater.

Not knowing that Vincenzo had died, Franco thought the monk's words were meant for him. The incident had one result: Franco no longer spent his idle hours in the piazza. He took to sitting on the road just outside his house. There he held forth to sympathetic listeners. He would admit nothing further to Father Giovanni, who wanted him to sign a testimony that would travel up the church hierarchy.

From his new location Franco was pressed by visitors inquiring about his vision. He answered their questions ambiguously. He wasn't sure whether he'd seen the monk's hood or not. As for the words, he'd heard them, but not clearly. This was enough to excite imaginations, and to satisfy Franco that he was getting even with Father Giovanni at last.

Franco was gradually sought by those with misfortunes and maladies usually presented to witches and priests: impotent husbands, barren wombs, the evil eye, jaundiced children. His dispensations were delivered with an inebriated callousness, for he was a heavy drinker as well as a cynic. He constantly warned that he possessed no special powers, but this warning had the opposite effect than he intended. Yet even in his drunkenness he protested that his cures were common knowledge, drawn from the bank of lore and superstition known to all: wear a red dress to ward off spells; bake menstrual blood into bread to quicken a husband or attract a lover; throw down salt before a witch's house; and for any unheard-of misfortune, rub salt and olive oil on the afflicted part.

One day when Santo went to call his father for supper, he saw a horse drawn cart stopped on the road. It was a bright yellow cart decorated with images from Sicilian myth. The horse was a lively animal whose bobbing head was topped with a feather plume.

An older couple sat in the cart. The woman had white hair and sallow skin. Her face was flat and oval, her lips colorless, her eyes without focus. Uncovered for Santo's father to inspect was a goiter the size of a small melon hanging from her neck. The husband was a sulfur mine worker who stank from his work, his face patterned with dirt-filled lines that might have been cut with a knife. He was unwrapping two legs of cured ham as well as several lengths of salami, more meat than the Regina family ate in half a year.

"I can't help you," Santo's father was saying, looking away from the meat.

"Do you want something else? Do you want wine? You could trade this for wine, or I could bring you wine instead."

"You don't understand. I have no power. The stories about me are exaggerations, the way stories become different when they pass among people."

"But you saw the holy monk! You saw Gangiuseppe with your own eyes!"

"Who told you that?"

"Everyone! They say the monk pronounced you dead, and then gave you life, and that even for a few minutes you were actually dead."

"This is false, all of it. I never saw the monk, only what was perhaps the bottom of his gown."

"A gown is as good as a whole monk."

"Listen here, I said perhaps the bottom of his gown. It's true I heard his voice, but the words weren't clear, and in any case weren't for me. They were for an old fisherman who now rests in his grave."

With these words the woman made the sign of the cross and the man shrugged helplessly. They drove back downhill, the cartwheels creaking in the sunset.

"What can I do?" asked his father as Santo picked up the chair and balanced it on his head for the short walk home. He watched the cart sink into the stony distance, the horse's neck and plume bobbing between the couple's heads. Santo thought of the meat in the back: two hams cured in salt and still in their unshaven skins; and then the sausage, dried, wrinkled, coated with white mold and smelling of fennel and pepper, an aroma so pungent and promising of fulfillment that he would always remember the way his stomach contracted at the sight and smell.

Then he felt his father's gentle hand on his shoulder. "What are you thinking, Santo?"

"That you should have taken the meat." The conclusion seemed perfectly natural, but his father's blow knocked the chair out of his hands and he found himself flying after it. Luckily it broke his fall, or he would have landed face-first.

"We don't take advantage," he said.

When word of Franco's refusal of the meat was known, they called him a fool, but he'd already drawn a line between himself and his fellow Castellanese. After the incident with the ham and sausage he rarely left home, and turned away those who sought advice and cures. The rickety chair on which he'd once held court was moved to the balcony. Here he sat, gazing into the lower valleys with a sprig of mint in his mouth. He suffered from an ailment common to old men in which urination was painful. When this pain abated he would bitterly mock the ignorance of his fellow townsmen and speak of his vision, how the monk was suspended in midair and spoke with a bubbling sound as if from under water. At such times Franco seemed happily resigned to his own death, and sang out "O what an odor of Paradise!" whenever someone passed under the balcony.

He spent his last days asking death to come. Since wine worsened his pain, he continued drinking, hoping to bring it on. There were brief periods when the pain subsided and he would show Santo the photographs sent by Angelina.

"You must do as she did. Go to North America, South America, even Australia. But don't stay here. There will never be anything. I was never content here, and survived only by making a joke of the place. But a man can't eat his jokes, for they soon come up from his stomach and he tastes them again."

Santo felt his father's traits within him and his inheritance was a conviction that he was different from those around him. He would not accept the common fate. This meant that Nicolo would be dealt with in a way both he and Santo were yet to discover.

After waiting in the tower for some time without seeing Nicolo, Santo rode up to the land that had sustained the family for so many years. The plot was a hundred paces long, and about half as wide, sloping up to a rock face. There were enough vines for a single barrel of wine, some space for beans and vegetables, but not enough to carry his family through the winter.

He sat in the shade of the rock and looked down over the vines growing on trellises of poles and sticks. The adjacent plots, which belonged to neighbors, were the same poor holdings: they had to be planted late because of the long winters.

Now Simone made his way up the terraced paths, leading his goat. Simone owned several holdings, including one next to Santo's. A man like this, whose property came from wealthy generations and lucky marriages, had no need of L'America.

"Ha!" said Simone, looking up from below. "I told you in L'America they would boot you in the ass and send you home. Now, admit you were foolish to leave all this." He indicated the green and gold cropped hills and valleys. "Look what happened to you over there. Nothing but trouble. The word has been passed along. And whether right or wrong, you've earned yourself a reputation. Have these peasants begun to kiss your hand?"

"Why should men kiss my hand?"

"L'America!" cried Simone, as if pleading with it. "There will be more killing than in Sicily. There's more to fight over." He wiped his face with a bandanna and said, "But there's trouble enough right here." He patted the younger man's knee playfully, then held up his hand in the sign of a pistol. "If you can do it over there, you can do it here."

"What did I do in L'America?"

Simone raised his eyebrows as if the answer were obvious. "Yours are the words of a modest man, and perhaps the story is untrue. But what people think you did is more important than what actually happened. Already they tell how some *padrone* went to another life."

Simone drew up his goat and began to squeeze its only productive teat, squirting the milk into his open mouth. Satisfied with the taste, he squeezed a quantity into a small clay jug and passed it over. "A man cannot choose the insults he will take," he said, watching Santo drink. "Who knows what will happen."

"Nobody knows," said Santo, draining the jug at Simone's urging. He leaned back against the rock to let the sun heat his body. He listened to the hard music of goat's milk being squirted into the jug.

"Will you go back to L'America?"

"I think so."

"With the children?"

"With both children."

"Many men have gone since we last met. Several have already come back with money, calling it the most accursed place they've ever seen, as full of violence as La Sicilia. I think you'll go back at the right time."

"And when will that be?"

Simone paused to wipe his brow again, then stood up, looking down at the panoramic view, one that would beguile an outsider into thinking that all Sicilians loved the beauty of their land. "Men go to L'America because there's something here they want to forget. This may be the daily insult of poverty or some other thing. How often have you heard of men being killed on the day their enemies set off for another country? Most of these cases are personal feuds, like your own. This is God's way of giving justice. And once the man is gone, the police have less work to do. These cases are eventually processed in the courts as a form of comedy because the convicted men are no longer in the country."

Santo acknowledged this advice with gestures indicating that he agreed with it. But did Simone realize that if he killed Nicolo, he'd have to go to L'America and kill the brother too? And would it change Mariana's condition? Not one bit.

"Over there I met the men from Palermo who sent that boss to another life. Such men kill without thinking, for the smallest offense is a question of life and death. Decisions are easy for them. And then I met another man, one who knew how to hold himself above these others; and yet when he needed to do his work, it was somehow done. The question is, what kind of man are you looking at now?"

"A man who thinks," said Simone. "But perhaps too much. Remember that nobody will miss the little worm who offended you."

CHAPTER 17

Mariana grew rapidly. Yet none in the family would witness the later stages of her pregnancy. In accord with Santo's plan she was taken to Palermo to live with a cousin named Strufolino, a candy maker. She spent her days shelling almonds and hazelnuts. These were ground into powder and mixed into a pot of cooking chocolate, which imparted a warm, sweet smell to the little house in a poor district of the city.

Strufolino was a fat man whose stomach stretched his trousers to the limit, and whose genitals were plainly outlined. He was a talkative fellow who regarded his sense of humor as curative.

"Where is your lover now?" he asked one day, patting Mariana's stomach. And he would make a sign with his flattened hands that meant "escape," bringing the upper edge of one hand against the palm of the other.

"He'll come," said Mariana, popping an almond into her mouth with confidence. "He'll come and take me to L'America."

Strufolino intended his teasing to prepare Mariana for disappointments to come: the loss of Nicolo and the surrender of her child. The glow of pregnancy still fueled her love, but when the child was gone, what then?

But his teasing also kept Nicolo's name alive. Mariana still believed her lover would come for her. He couldn't be happy with his new wife. No other woman could do what she'd done. None could open him up like she did.

"Tell me," said Strufolino. "Why hasn't this young man come for you already? Why aren't you in L'America right now picking up the coins thrown in the streets by the rich?"

"Because he knows my father will follow us."

Strufolino dismissed her with a short laugh. "Nicolo isn't afraid of your father. Such men don't fear for their safety, for they're born under the protection of others. In his case, not only a father who is friendly with men of influence, but a brother in L'America besides—Carmeluzzo—a dangerous man who learned his business in the hills. They say he returns to Sicily in secret to murder those who might take revenge on his family for the crimes he once committed." And here

Strufolino made a sign that meant "death," or the finality of something, turning his palm up and moving it in a circle.

One night Strufolino said, "Come, I will show you the man who loves you."

He took Mariana to that part of the city known for its bordellos, where they knocked on the door of a woman's apartment. The woman had short blond hair and a complexion so pale that Mariana wanted to tell her to drink more wine. She dismissed Strufolino and placed Mariana inside a closet with a peephole that looked into the room where the business was done. She instructed Mariana to be silent, then went out the door and reappeared in the room where she sat on the bed and waited. Nicolo soon entered, his small black eyes rolling warily. Standing before her, he removed his shoes and trousers, then submitted to inspection and washing.

In the next few moments the detachment that Mariana tried to summon changed to a revulsion so nauseating that she left the closet. She opened a window in another part of the apartment and took deep breaths of the night air. Something private and sacred had turned grotesque and shameless. Later the woman returned to the apartment. She sat Mariana down and poured two glasses of red-colored *liquore*. She introduced herself as Andrea. When Mariana didn't respond, the woman shrugged and drank, closing her large, dark eyes as soon as the glass touched her lips. She drained the glass, poured another, then looked up and said, "So what do you think?" Andrea had the same frightened look as Giuseppina from the laundry pool. "That wasn't very nice to see, was it."

Mariana shook her head.

"Come on, take a drink. It will settle your stomach. You want to know how I do it? I'll tell you how. You have three children and no husband and no money, then you'll see how it's done."

She lifted one bony arm to drink again. "Your man is nothing special. One little thing excites him. With him it's my blond hair, which is dyed, everywhere. My hair reminds him of a story he heard as a boy about a princess. Men are all the same. In a rut they'll put it anywhere. They want nothing to do with emotions, they simply need sensation in that part between the legs—all body and no mind. And in order to have it they'll pay quite a bit."

Andrea finished her drink, then unhitched her stockings and rolled them part way down her thighs.

"Then you're convinced?" she asked.

"Of what?"

"That he's the kind of man I say and nothing special?"

Mariana never answered the question. If all men were like that, what was the difference? Whores, however, didn't provide love. Within days, like rain filling a dry stream, Nicolo's love flooded back into her breast. Through the hours of birthing pains while pitiless nuns circled her bed like crows, she rationalized his visit to the blond-haired prostitute: he'd done it because his wife couldn't please him and because he missed his true love. And when the labor pains made her want to curse him for the human creature breaking out of her body with the force of a storm, the pious arrogance of the nuns helped her bear the pain.

"This is the price you pay for your sins," they said.

So she gave birth with cries of double anguish, and this prolonged pain transported her to a world where she no longer had to think, but merely to breathe, to gasp, until the rhythm of her desire to breathe and her desire to expel this child worked together with the force of her will. Then she pushed hard, no longer caring if her insides were lost.

The child was lifted away and never seen again. She wasn't allowed to hold it, nor was she told whether it was male or female. She saw a heavy covering of dark hair, then a tiny, glistening creature that flew out of sight.

CHAPTER 18

Mariana sat in the basement drinking chamomile tea and holding back her tears. Franco was arranging the hand-tied hay bales he'd cut on the roadside that day. He was fifteen now, and in her absence he'd lost his little boy's look and had broken out in facial hair and muscles on his arms. While stacking the bales he told her the latest news, that Nicolo had moved back to Castellano with his wife.

In order to spare her embarrassment at the news, Franco continued working with the bales, trying not to look into his sister's face. But he couldn't avoid seeing her tears. Sitting beside her, he took the teacup from her hand and gave her a handkerchief to dry her eyes. Mariana felt strength from him now, some of that strength imparted by his budding manhood, but most by his resemblance to their mother, who had been the strength of the family until she died. Like their mother, Franco had a prominent nose, and when he was a boy that nose looked soft and vulnerable; but now, because of maturity, his facial expression was sharp and aggressive.

"I don't care if he's back here," said Mariana.

"He passes the house every morning, like before."

"I know that and I don't care."

Franco said, "We're going to L'America anyway. But just before that . . ." He finished the sentence by making a pistol sign with his hand, aiming it at an imaginary moving target, and then pulling the trigger. "Once in L'America what happened here no longer matters," he said. "Or what is about to happen."

He touched her hand tentatively, then gave her a signal to pay attention and remain silent. He opened the cellar door to allow light to enter. Then he reached into a saddle pouch hidden under some straw and took out a long-barreled pistol, holding it up for Mariana to see.

"I know how to use it too," he said. "Father taught me."

"Why did he teach you?"

"Who knows? Maybe he thinks the Infante family will someday kill him."

"Afterward?"

"After he kills Nicolo."

"How do you know he's going to do that?"

"Because he wears a pistol all the time now, and Nonna told me he won't hesitate to use it. He's done it before, in L'America." Franco sighted down the pistol barrel. "They say he killed a boss who cheated him."

He pulled the trigger and the hammer clicked. Mariana felt a stab in her heart. Such easy talk of killing, as if it were part of growing up in the world, a skill acquired in adulthood by those fit for it, as some women were more fit for baking bread than others. Here she sat with milk hardening in her breasts, her insides raw from a child being ripped away, and faced with the prospect of seeing Nicolo again—a daily reminder of the insult.

"Do they kill so easily in L'America?"

"The bosses beat the Sicilians with whips if they don't work hard enough. Then they cheat them of their pay. This was why he came home so late. He needed to get a second job because he was cheated."

"Then why are we going to L'America if he killed a man there? Won't the police be looking for him?"

Franco laughed. "L'America is so big that you can kill twenty men and the police wouldn't care."

He held the pistol close to his ear and with a well-practiced motion turned the chamber to hear the clicks.

"We'll live in New York City near Angelina. But even if nothing happens to us here, we'll still be in danger afterwards because Nicolo's brother also lives in New York. Father will have to kill the brother too. Do you know about the brother?"

She answered his question only with her eyes. Of course she knew about the brother. Franco then rested the pistol against a horizontal beam and aimed at various objects in the cellar. Then he climbed the stack of hay bundles near the window and poking the pistol between some window bars he pretended to fire.

"From here I can hit a man at the gate, but not in the road. The road is too far for the pistol. If I want to hit a man in the road, I must hide behind the gate, near the stone wall, like this!" He jumped from the hay pile and sprang over to the cart, aiming the pistol between the wheel spokes. Then he looked up to Mariana and said, "I'm glad you're back. Now we can kill that man who betrayed you and go to L'America."

Mariana climbed up on the cart seat and looked around the small room. She saw that the cellar door was locked with a heavy sapling pole. The fear of the unknown was more profound now than when she was pregnant. She'd come back home with the hope that all would be forgotten, even forgiven, not perhaps between her father and Nicolo, but between her father and herself. She believed that the ordeal of birth and the loss of her child was the price her father would accept for his forgiveness. But that hadn't come.

The responsibility to rescue her honor lay with her, not with her father. And the opportunity was there. Nicolo, the father of their lost child, rode by the house every day on that mule with the copper-colored nose. What did he care about the child, or about her? There he was, as before, wearing his old black cap low on his eyes to give the impression that he was sleeping. He no longer looked for Mariana, not since her father had come home. He clip-clopped past as if the insult and pain she'd borne, the kicking child in her stomach, the complication of blood and organs that were part of its birth, had never been a reality.

And this man pretending to sleep in the saddle, had eaten, breathed, and whored while she lay groaning on an orphanage bed expelling their child. Nor did he know of that other pain when the child was snatched away. He knew nothing and cared less about what it felt like to carry another human being inside her body, to feel it kick and move its arms, to hear it talk—or to imagine it talking. And then to give it up.

One morning before sunrise she went to the gate and began draping laundry over the bars. She wore a pretty smock and had wrapped her head in a print bandanna sent by Angelina. When Nicolo came up close she set the bundle of laundry down and placed one hand on her hip to entice him.

Did he think the old game would resume? Did he consider that laundry was rarely hung out before the sun came up? But now his eyes flickered and he smiled. That was perfect. Did he know that Franco had taught her to fire the pistol? Did he know that as soon as he passed by, she would pull out the pistol hidden in the laundry?

He knew none of this. He did not see her aim the pistol through the bars of the gate. When she pulled the trigger, it was doubtful he heard the shot that spooked his mule and sent his cap flying into the weeds with part of his brains and skull.

CHAPTER 19

In the basement where the two mules were tied, Santo strapped a valise onto his own mule and hung the *lupara* over the saddle. There was money in his pocket and food in a sack. A steamship waited in Palermo, and once again he would cross the ocean, but this time as a man who'd killed twice even though he hadn't killed anyone—not that boss in Louisiana, not that *bastardo* whose body was draped over the other mule. Now his reputation would precede him and there would be consequences enough. He could only hope that by the time Nicolo's body was found he'd be walking the streets of New York City.

As a farewell to home he climbed the ladder to his room and opened a pressboard trunk. He felt the handmade lacework, the embroidered sheets and baby clothes made for grandchildren, all this for a happy future. He slid his hands between the items to coat them with the touch of his wife's hands. There was a clean dryness there, a purity of new cotton associated not only with her but with the sacraments of their former life as well. He would never see these again. He closed the trunk and went down to the kitchen. Mariana and his mother huddled in the semidarkness. Mariana was crying.

His mother took his arm. "Talk to her before you go away. Don't make her more miserable than she is already."

He stood in front of Mariana, who shook with relentless, intermittent sobbing.

"Look at me."

"I can't."

"That was my work to do, not yours!" He shook her until she looked up at him. "Am I Jesus Christ that I can pretend this has never happened, or that I can forgive what you've done? All our lives are in danger now instead of only mine!"

He called Franco up from the cellar and spoke to both of them. "Now, do as I say or there's no hope. Tell them I've gone to Australia, or maybe Canada, you don't know where. And when you receive word from Angelina, come to New York."

He went to the basement where Nicolo's mule was tied. Franco came down and held the mule's halter to keep it calm. It had stamped the ground beneath it to mud. It was spooked, not only by new surroundings, but also by its burden: Nicolo's body, rolled in a blanket and covered with hay.

Santo called Mariana down and she stood there not crying anymore but looking at him directly. Her blue eyes were forceful, like those of her mother.

Santo asked, "Did you think I would be proud of you for this?"

She looked up. Her eyes rolled slightly, incredulous. He of all people would know the answer to that question. She turned her eyes downward again.

"Answer me!"

She looked up again, with even more disbelief in her eyes, which didn't roll this time, but which challenged him. "Yes, I thought you would be proud." She cried into her hands.

Santo turned to Franco. The boy wasn't innocent either. "You!" He slapped him on top of the head. "Am I a magician who makes dead men disappear? Now I must hide him until the stink of his corpse attracts the wolves and dogs. Did this come into your mind when you gave her that pistol? Tell me, how can you be so stupid as to kill a man in front of your own house?"

Franco looked at his feet. Mariana continued sobbing.

"Give her some water," he said to Franco.

Her eyes fixed him while she drank. He gestured toward the body. "Did you think this *cafone* would fly away by himself after you killed him? Or that his animal wouldn't be found wandering the road?"

"We planned to take him away," said Franco.

"Both of you? To carry him off like a bundle of sticks?"

"There are caves nearby and the old salt mine," said Franco. "The mine is on the way to Palermo, and we're still packed for L'America. We could all go together. The police won't come looking until they find his body. That might be months, or even years."

Santo looked from one to the other. Mariana had stopped crying. Franco looked at him now. They were proud of themselves. "And what am I supposed to do with him?"

"I can show you the place we were speaking about," said Franco.

"And take the risk of being discovered while hiding him? Or that by our disappearance all three of us will be charged with his murder? Until they find his corpse the *carabinieri* will be faced with only two missing men. They won't know which of us is dead or alive. You must behave as if you're free of suspicion. You know nothing of dead men."

"Do you know about his brother?" asked Franco.

"Yes. The great Carmeluzzo."

"When we come to L'America we can help."

"Help with what."

"With him."

He didn't hit the boy hard, but hard enough to make his teeth click together.

"Remember me by that."

CHAPTER 20

Santo followed a trail along a slope with rock outcroppings that seemed ready to fall. The sky was hazy, the stars without luster. A cloud scurried under the moon and darkened the landscape. Santo turned to look at Castellano one last time. It was a giant tooth, its chalky crown facing skyward and ghostly in the night.

He was seeing this country for the last time, and as he surveyed this semi-barren region with its lunar mountains, he wished there were no need to be quiet. He wanted to fling his most bitter curses at it. Sicily had given him nothing but defeats—his wife's death, his fruitless embrace of Don Vito's ideas, his failure to do something about Nicolo, and a blindness to Mariana's feelings. Now the course of his life was being dictated by the daughter who'd shown him up as indecisive when his plan had been to wait until he'd sent his family on to L'America. Then he would have dealt with Nicolo. He spat on the ground to get the bitterness out of his mouth.

There was one consolation: L'America. In Sicily he would have slept his life away on a mule's back. He would have been an ant, bringing bits of food from field to home, putting roughage into one end of an animal and carrying off what came out the other. He would trudge through life with the memory of beans thrown in his face until his eyes and soul developed a glaze of indifference. He would look at his enemies and see nothing.

The night brightened. He passed estates and clusters of houses. He skirted sleeping villages too small for names, places where people lived with some reduced metabolism, like animals in winter. He would be in Bagheria by daylight, Palermo before noon. Nicolo's mule followed calmly now. The hay made a rustling sound.

Santo came to a stone tower where he dismounted and led both animals inside. This tower had a ladder reaching to the top, the circular stairs on the inside having long collapsed into rubble. He moved enough stone to make a body-sized impression, then tried to set Nicolo into it. But the body had assumed the curve of the mule's back. Rather than try to straighten it, he removed more stones and lay it down on its side. He spread the blanket as best he could and made sure the head was covered.

So it's happened. Whether he or Mariana had killed Nicolo, the result was the same: this would define his life. When he died they would speak of him in terms of this event. Nothing would be greater—no accomplishment, no act, no labor. He covered the body with stones, piling them high.

CHAPTER 21

In 1907 the Bureau of Immigration at Ellis Island processed more Italian immigrants than ever before. Over a quarter of a million Italians, mostly from the south, arrived in steamships that often waited in the harbor for days before passengers could disembark. The immigration staff tried to weed out the infirm, the old, those without prospects, the criminals, the insane, sometimes even the illiterate. Their first test was a visual inspection, which began when the immigrants carried their luggage up a flight of steps past a group of doctors and officials who watched closely. Those who climbed the steps without obvious discomfort were considered to have passed the medical test. Those having difficulty were checked further. Once admitted to the country, the immigrant was ferried to the railroad station on the New Jersey shore, or to the Barge Office in Battery Park. The area outside this office was crowded with boarding house agents, representatives of benevolent societies, and hustlers of all kinds.

Santo moved quickly through this crowd and into the street, observing how many new arrivals were taken in by the various agents, and especially the *padroni*, who held up contracts and called out the daily wage: the same tactic used on the steamship to New Orleans. The bosses were transparent but effective. Their strategy was to gain the confidence of the disoriented newcomer by claiming associations to the same part of Italy. These men had cousins in every town from Sicily to Switzerland, and the new immigrants often succumbed to the schemes presented. They were desperate and pragmatic. They wanted to get settled as quickly as possible since many of them wanted to make some money and go back home.

What Santo had seen in New Orleans was a trickle. This was a deluge—not only from Italy, but the northern European countries as well. It seemed as if one side of the earth had tipped into the other. These were weary men and women—pale, sick, proud, sitting on benches with puzzled looks on their faces, some of them crying and laughing in the arms of already settled relatives. Some had their belongings in valises, baskets, pillowcases, in bags sewn from fishnet. Here was a woman with pots and pans on a rope around her neck, there a group of Italians dancing and singing to accordion and mandolin.

Santo was tempted to intervene for the more vulnerable ones, those waylaid by one thief or another. In other circumstances he would have done more to help, but he had to think of himself now. A persistent fear had driven him quickly through the Barge Office and into the nearby streets where the scene was repeated with even more intensity. Here, away from the not-so-wary eye of immigration officials were flocks of men selling insurance, banking services, return tickets, jobs, food, and stationery with no extra charge for writing services. Ignoring those who approached him, Santo made his way to the elevated train station at South Ferry and took the train to the Fulton Street market. From there he planned to walk to his sister's house.

The elevated train seemed to fly, but not smoothly. It was a rocking steel car screeching on steel tracks and old timbers, and the thought of the whole structure collapsing into the crowded streets below gave rise to a feeling of danger, but also discovery. This is what L'America would be like. He could see clear across the boat-filled harbor to bodies of land east and west, whether mainland or more islands he couldn't tell. The land across the water was partly forested. From what he already knew, there was room for enough people to make the flood he'd seen at Ellis Island appear as a drop.

Could Carmelo Infante find him here? Could he locate one Sicilian in a city stuffed with immigrants like a tin of anchovies? The streets below the rickety track were choked with pushcarts, peddlers, horse-drawn vehicles, an occasional motorcar belching smoke. All kinds of goods were moving: lumber, bricks, barrels, ice, fruit, hanging meat, clothing. There were hungry people in those streets too, rag pickers and children born to a life of thievery. But most of all there was activity. He could smell work. He could smell the idea that a man could sell something—even the clothes off his back—and make enough money to keep going.

At the Fulton market he passed among the fish stalls and vendors' carts and bought an orange. He found an empty crate on the pier's edge and sat down. The orange was from Florida. It was big and pale. There was a place near home called Tarocco where the sweetest oranges were grown. The flesh of a Tarocco orange was blood red, and the rind came off in a single piece. A baby could peel one. Santo smelled his American orange. The fragrance was sharp, not sweet. He would make the best of it. He would adjust to L'America. He was about to peel his Florida orange when he looked up to a tugboat steaming down the river with a crew of shirtless men sitting on the deck smoking pipes and cigars. An eye was painted on the prow of the boat, above it the name Tonnara. A Sicilian town, the eye was a Sicilian sign. The Italians were here, they were making their way, and Santo suddenly felt, as in New Orleans, overpowered and behind the progress he should be making. He was thinking about oranges while the world—even the Italian world—ran ahead of him. He was thinking about oranges when at this very moment his family could be in jail, suffering the indignities of Sicilian law.

Behind him the market rang with the violence of trade: Fish sellers were bargaining with customers. Not all the voices were Italian. He listened to the efforts of buyer and seller to find a common language. Some of the Italians already knew Yiddish, German, and English. In the rush of this life, how could the police, the immigration, or even Carmelo Infante locate a Sicilian in rough wool clothes who resembled so many others? He resolved to cover his fears with confidence. Back in Louisiana, William and Vaccarella had shown him that L'America was dangerous but free. Its advantages for the immigrant were size and scale. He could sell fish or fruit tomorrow. He could sell the orange in his hand for a penny profit and buy two more and sell those. He could have a business or build track on the railroad, a job advertised in the windows of the agencies he passed. This city belonged as much to him as the others, and knowing Italians and their exaggerated sense of intrigue, the best place to hide would be in the open.

"Regina! Santo Regina!"

He didn't move. There could be another with the same name. The name was common enough. Pretending not to hear, he studied the murky water and its floating garbage.

"Regina from Castellano!" The accent was Sicilian.

Still he didn't look up, but continued to focus on the river until he felt a presence and shifted his eyes to a pair of shoes with leather so worn that every toe was outlined. The shoes had been polished so many times that wax had built up like shingles. Above the shoes were a soiled, mouse-colored suit and a black sweater riddled with moth holes. This covering of old clothes contained a worried, unshaven fellow with hollow cheeks, and a once-broken nose pushed to one side. And like that of a cruising fish, his mouth was unable to close over his large teeth, which seemed to consist only of the upper row.

It was Paolo Nerone, a friend from Palermo.

"What are you doing here?" asked Santo.

"The same as everyone else. And some saint is watching over you, Regina. Some saint manipulates steamships, people, even the elements to make life go your way. I left Palermo on the *Perugia* one week after you, and since we encountered no storms, we disembarked the same time as you. You don't know this, but I've been watching you from the moment you arrived at the *Batteria*."

Like a woman lifting a skirt, Nerone took hold of his jacket and hiked it up before squatting down so he could be level with Santo. "Knowing I was coming to L'America, Strufolino sent me to warn you. And had I not seen your ship in the harbor, I would have gone straight to your sister's house. Instead I hurried to see you, then to be safe, I followed you here on the incredible flying train instead of approaching you directly.

"Now, believe me, Santo, I know nothing of your trouble. Of this I swear by everything holy. I have only this message from Strufolino: Whatever has happened is 'Known by everyone!' Those were his words, 'Known by everyone.' He said you would understand the meaning, and was afraid to write you a letter because the police might open it."

"And my children?"

"They arrive shortly."

Santo dug his thumb into the orange and removed the skin in short ribbons. The pulp of this American orange was pale and watery. "Known by everyone." What did that mean? Did they know his daughter had killed Nicolo? Or did they merely know that Nicolo was dead? The news intensified that small, persistent irritation he carried with him. He looked at Paolo and said, "The trouble isn't serious, a matter of property, no more. And I have no fear of those who may be against me. My cousin likes to worry. But tell me, Paolo," he said, relaxing his tone to dismiss the subject, "Why did you come here? I thought you were doing well at home?"

"What man does well in Sicily?" replied Paolo. In Palermo he'd been a *Padrone di Bordello*, and the man to consult for female problems. At his disposal was a network of prostitutes, doctors, and women who could perform abortions and treat female sickness and complaints.

Santo could see why Strufolino trusted Paolo. The young man's physical ugliness was matched by a willingness to work to overcome that drawback. His cunning and honesty combined to give an impression of innocence. But Paolo was far from innocent. He was sly, eager, accommodating.

Paolo lit a small cigar and blew the smoke at the ground. Then he spat. "There's nothing in Sicily."

"What will you do here?"

"Let me tell you something, my friend. The man you knew in Palermo wasn't what he seemed, not a fast talker in fine clothes, but a small boy kept by a mother with a large house near the Corso. I was a *caruso*, a cleaning boy, one who swept the floor, changed the beds, kept an eye out, even hawked for business in the street. My only pay was something to eat and a roof over my head.

"Do you know what I did for money? I worked at the only trade I knew—whores. I would find a young girl with a little trust left in her soul, one who hadn't been milked dry by life near the piers. I would go after her like a lovesick boy and swear I couldn't afford to pay for a night's services. Some would give in. Then I would appear with money and a sad story of how I sacrificed to get it. The guard would fall even further. She would take me to her room. And when the moment was ripe, when she fell asleep after the ecstasy of love, I would steal whatever I could, including the money I'd just paid, of course.

"Once I played this trick on the wrong girl. Two men came and trussed me up and carried me out to the country. They began to cut my throat, but seeing I was young, and partly believing my tale of woe, they didn't slit it seriously enough to kill me, only to teach me a lesson. They left me bleeding nearly to death, but eventually I made my way back to the city.

"After that I came to L'America. Two times I've been here, once in New Jersey where I had to push a wheelbarrow full of cement so heavy that the muscles of my stomach nearly broke through my skin. Each time I swore never to come back. Yet here I am. But now it will be different. This is another reason why I consented to deliver this message to you. You always appeared to be a man with different ideas, a man who might know how to make his way. Look around you, business everywhere! Why don't we do something together?"

Santo finished the orange and wiped his mouth with a handkerchief. "It puzzles me when you say I'm a certain kind of man, one with special abilities to make money, as if I have some secret, or some influence. Believe me, I know nothing. I work with my hands, just like you. There's no difference between me and thousands of others filling the steamships. Why do you have this opinion of me? What have you heard?"

Paolo's eyes, wide with amazement, looked in two different directions. "A man doesn't leave for L'America without his children unless something's wrong. I don't care what happened to you in Sicily, or over here for that matter. Yet I don't want to hold anything back, otherwise it would be hard to look you in the eye. I've been told that you worked on a crew in Louisiana whose boss was killed, a man named Torino who deserved death ten times over."

"Who told you this story?"

A *mariolo* named Zillo, now in L'America, where he continues his former work."

"Did he tell you I killed that boss?"

"Not in so many words."

"But you believe it."

In Paolo's shrug Santo read the answer. This was good. If Paolo believed the story about Torino, he would believe the same of Nicolo.

"I know what you're thinking," said Paolo. "And I know more than you think. When you sent your daughter to Strufolino he consulted me at once, knowing I might have ways to solve the problem. He did this because he knew I could be trusted.

"Now," continued Paolo, as if giving lessons which had to be explained step by step, "It doesn't matter to me whether you killed

Nicolo Infante or even that *padrone* in New Orleans. I know what these men inflict on our countrymen. Now tell me, do we work together or not?"

"I'll think about it."

He shook hands with Paolo and started for his sister's house, but he was soon lost in the crowded streets. He hadn't expected a city so full of non-Italians as well. Certain streets were boundaries between nationalities, or between southern Italians with different dialects. At a certain point he passed into an area where western Sicilian dialects jumped at him from everywhere. He might have been walking through the center of Palermo, or even Castellano. Men who sounded like his neighbors were hawking their goods. There were storefront clubs from small Sicilian towns, societies named after various saints, and a discouraging number of vendors using carts, basins, baskets, even small buckets to display seafood. Could all these people earn a living? The uncomfortable fear he'd felt at the fish market was suddenly present again, and he decided not to buy some pastries for his sister as a homecoming gift. The purchase might require a discussion with someone from his region.

He walked from Canal to Elizabeth Street, no longer lost, but not stopping at the address where Angelina lived. Her street was like the others, with stores under tenements. Some of the buildings were old and falling apart, some newer and made of brick. The street was nearly choked to traffic by lines of carts, pushed or horse-drawn. The men and women calling to one another from the buildings or calling to groups of children seemed content with their surroundings. This made him feel better. He felt excited at the sound of his dialect, and as much as he didn't want to be discovered, he found himself looking for familiar faces.

CHAPTER 22

The doctor was an older woman wearing a stethoscope and holding a black satchel open to various instruments. She spoke to Mariana in Italian. "*Signorina*, I beg you, submit to this examination. There will be only myself and a nurse. We mean absolutely no harm."

Nobody had warned Mariana about this. She'd been told by Strufolino to reveal only her name, age, home town, and the address of an aunt who would pick her up. She was to say that her parents were dead. She was to show the lira equivalent of seventeen dollars to prove she was self-supporting. She would consent to various superficial medical inspections, those for eyes, ears, mouth, and skin. But nothing had been said about going into a room and removing all her clothes while this woman did God-knows-what with the tools in her satchel.

"My dear *Signorina*, this is the law! Please, there's nothing to be afraid of." The doctor had been standing with the inspectors observing the immigrants carrying their baggage up the steps from the boat landing. They'd singled out Mariana even though she'd swept up the steps ahead of her group. Young girls traveling alone were checked for venereal disease.

Mariana tried to appear confident. She set her bag between her feet and put her hands on her hips. She assumed a skeptical and resentful look. This could be a test of another kind: if she submitted to this inspection too easily, they might think she was a *puttana* because she was accustomed to showing herself. Then they'd surely send her home.

"No," she said, speaking for the first time. "I cannot do this. You can speak about it with my aunt."

To her surprise the doctor wasn't angered by this refusal. She guided Mariana to a railed enclosure, and told her to wait. Mariana sat on a bench and wondered if she'd convinced the doctor that she was clean enough to be an American. She leaned back, supporting her head on the iron bars of the enclosure. She wanted to sleep but couldn't take her eyes off her travel bag, a double pillowcase reinforced with pieces of coarse cotton at the corners. Sewing that bag had provided her with hours of pleasure. While pulling the stitches tight she imagined every step of her journey and the hardships the bag would have to endure.

From her coat pocket she removed the photograph of Angelina that she was to show the immigration officials. The photograph showed the aunt on the street in New York City, obviously clowning, wearing an apron and a flowered hat, her face turned in profile, her tongue touching the tip of a hooked nose that was so uncharacteristic of the Regina family.

Mariana had refused, against Strufolino's instructions, to pin the photo on her coat. Only the greenest, most backward Italians used this trick. The photo would stay in her pocket. She gripped the bag with her feet and looked around the great receiving room at Ellis Island. Strufolino had repeatedly told her that she wouldn't be out of danger until after a second ferry ride to a place called the *Batteria*. Even there an official might question her, whether to determine if she knew any English—which would work in her favor—or for another reason. She and Strufolino had practiced for hours:

"What is your name?"

"Maria Savino."

"Good! How old are you?"

"*I emma seek-es-teen!*"

A young girl sitting beside Mariana kept a bag of bright rags between her feet. She was sewing these into flowers. Her deft fingers sewed two or three strips of rag to a wire and fashioned flower petals with a pair of scissors. While working she spoke to herself in Neapolitan dialect, of which Mariana had heard a great deal on the ship. The Neapolitans were incessant talkers, outgoing, even comical, unable to keep secrets, taking her in as one of their own, even pointing out the thieves among their own kind for her benefit.

The flower girl turned to Mariana and said, "Were you on the *Lombardia*?" She didn't wait for an answer. "I don't think so because I didn't see you. I would have noticed because your hair was so long and black, very black, my dear. Perhaps you were on the *Perugia*. This must be your first trip, I can tell by the way you look around. I myself go back and forth like a swallow. I earn money from these flowers and bring it back to my family in Posillipo. I never send money. They steal it from the mail. Do you see these flowers? I learned how to make them from a Jewish woman on Grand Street. She said they would make me rich. They are easy to make. But my eyes are so bad I must look closer all the time. Soon I will earn enough to buy eyeglasses. I worked for this woman's husband putting pockets and seams on dresses. He liked the way I made coffee, nice and strong, Italian style. What will you do in L'America, my dear?"

Lightly, and for security, Mariana touched the string of the Saint Peter's scapular around her neck to which a silk purse containing her money had been sewn. She gave the string a tug and checked the purse between her breasts.

"I'm going to be an opera singer," Mariana replied. It was something she'd overheard another woman saying on the steamship.

"Truly!" replied the other with no trace of disbelief, as if being an opera singer were as easy as sewing flowers from rags. Her ingenuous tone of voice gave Mariana a pleasant feeling to counter the disorder around her. Nearby an old man was dabbing his eyes with a handkerchief because he hadn't been admitted. There was violin music in the distance. Immigrants kept watch on their baggage of burlap sacks and satchels worn to cardboard and tied with twine. One man's goods were stuffed into a pair of trousers, which leaned against a pillar like part of a corpse. Families argued with immigration officials while trying to keep unruly youngsters in tow.

"L'America is a good place for singers," said the girl. "There are many small opera houses where you can work. And of course there's the grand opera, where you can hear the great ones. I know this because I sell my flowers outside such places. My name is Cimarosa, Olga. What is your name, my dear?"

"Savino, Maria."

The name was still clumsy to say, but once it passed her lips she leaned back and rested her eyes on the gray light from the surrounding windows. She wasn't really here in this great room with its high ceiling. Only her body was in L'America. Back in Castellano a mule tapped its greeting on the road and Nicolo came into view, his hat pulled over his eyes. He wasn't pretending to be asleep at all, but in a state he'd once described to her as "the stupor of the peasant."

Even now she wondered if she should have played the martyr and taken him back; but on his last day, when his eyes flickered toward the house as if to say, "There lives the *puttana* whose love meant nothing," he placed himself in the hands of death.

But if she could kill him, had she really loved him? And what had she loved? Perhaps not him so much as herself, or what she became with him, powerful, the only woman who could make him whimper like a child; the only woman who could tame that impulsive creature living inside him. Spent, he clung like a baby, no bragging about L'America, no ridiculous promises. Like a calm sea he spoke of fruits and vegetables, the rustle of water, the moods of his mule, the quality of the wheat grown on his land.

But then the "fish" would rule him once more. Aroused, he would demand that she repeat her love and loyalty, not to him but to the instrument of his love: "Don't say you love *me*, say you love *this*!" And she said it, with all the ardor he demanded, for that was her power. She let him play her like an instrument because her submission was a path to her power. Now she recognized how foolish this was, and so for the child torn from her womb, for the insult to her family, for the pain to her father, Nicolo had paid the price. All that was clear now. What she couldn't understand was why her father, who'd killed a boss for less of an offense, didn't worship the ground she walked on now that she'd saved the family honor.

She heard Olga's voice. "Are you afraid, my dear? Afraid of this big country?"

"Why do you ask that?"

"Because you look so worried. Did something happen back home? Fear is a sign of intelligence. Here you will succeed, for let me tell you, the fear will go away. For a while you will want to go back home, but that will pass when you earn some money. You can get money here, but you must work harder than you ever worked at home. So you're from Palermo. That means you know the sea, like me. I love the sea. Here you can look at the sea but it's not the same. It is filthy. Maybe you miss your *fidanzato*? Do you have one? Mine hated it here. He had to break rocks with a hammer and went back to Posillipo because the work cut his hands. He didn't like the food. He didn't like the English. So let him go back to Posillipo! He's waiting for me, but he'll have a long wait. Another man wants me already. There are so many men here, but one must be careful. Sometimes they take what they want, then *Whoosh! Whoosh!* Do you know that kind?"

Olga bent over her work and continued speaking as some reddish hair loosened from her kerchief partially hid her face.

"My *fidanzato*, the first one, didn't like the Irish. They go around twenty and thirty at a time, they see one Italian, *Wop! Wop! Wop!* Then they try to kill him. So he carried a pistol to protect himself. He worked setting stones into Canal Street, but he cut his hands too often. He thought I would follow him home. So you are *palermitana*? You're dark like all Sicilians and with blue eyes like so many of them. And your man, where is he?"

She snipped some stray threads and wound the wire stem with bits of green and red cloth. After bringing it all together with a few stitches, she held it up for Mariana.

"You can pin it on your dress, on your hair, or put it in a pretty vase at home."

"No, I have no money."

"You must have five cents, or a few lira. I know because they wouldn't let you get this far. Everyone must have a certain amount of money or else they go back."

Mariana showed her empty hands.

"It doesn't matter. Take it, free, a gift for your new life. When you're a famous singer and I'm selling these flowers outside the opera house, you can pay me back. Then you can buy all my flowers and take me in as your maid. Come on, it's a beautiful flower for a beautiful girl."

"I can't."

"Listen, dear. Things are a little different over here. People give gifts even if it's not a feast day. Besides that, if anyone sees me take money for this flower, they may send me back because I have no *licenza*. Now, take this for good luck. Someone will see it and want one. And remember, if they ask, it was a gift. Now here's my sister-in-law," she said, pointing to a woman in a straw bonnet talking to an official.

"Maybe we'll meet again. Come on, take the flower! People here trust each other!"

The woman in the straw bonnet didn't speak, but waved her cane to direct Olga toward an exit where a ferry was loading passengers for the *Batteria*.

Watching Olga being herded into the crowd and funneled up the ferry gangplank made Mariana wonder if she would have a chance for a friend again. She even went so far as to project their friendship even further: she and Olga making flowers together, perhaps having a flower factory similar to Strufolino's candy shop, hiring single females like themselves to sell flowers in the streets. She could be a woman of business, just like her aunt.

The whistle and departure of the ferry reminded Mariana that perhaps Angelina had arrived on the same boat. So, best be ready to go, and try to ignore this trouble with the doctor. She reached for her bag, but it wasn't there.

Shame and frustration weakened her knees. The words of her elders had proven true. *Watch out for thieves*. She looked around; nothing and everything were suspicious. Then it came to her. Olga! She ran toward the gangplank but too late. The packed ferry churned away from the pier with a shrill whistle and the decks were jammed. Mariana could make out neither Olga nor the woman in the straw bonnet. The boat's name was *Pelican*, and while remembering this name for the immigration authorities, she felt for the scapular and silk purse, thinking that Olga's Neapolitan hands were bewitched enough to pull out her purse. But the money was still there, and had she not been in L'America she would have taken out the scapular and kissed Saint Peter's picture.

"What is it, my dear? Are you crying for home already?"

A tall woman held Mariana's bag in front of her like a shield. Her face was dark, her eyebrows dramatically furrowed, as if Mariana's inattention would merit retribution next time. Even with the silly photograph in her pocket, Mariana wouldn't have recognized her aunt. Angelina was still tall and rangy, but now thicker at the waist, her hair beginning to gray.

"Yes, it's me," she said, pushing the pillowcase into Mariana's arms to avoid an embrace. "No kisses now. This is a lesson to keep your eyes open. Sleeping on the bench! And next to that *napolitana*! Now let's hurry. Another ferry is about to leave. Your father, your brother, all safe for now. Just don't ask questions, especially when others can hear you."

"And that woman? The doctor?"

Angelina waved the matter away. "Don't worry, she's too busy to notice."

CHAPTER 23

Elizabeth Street was a crowded world of vendors, carts, and uncontrolled children. Everyone seemed to be yelling. Pedestrians choked the sidewalk and spilled into the street where they obstructed the traffic. Horse-drawn wagons were packed with peppers and eggplants and artichokes, giant apples and oranges, hanging goats and lambs, cages of chickens and squab, gobs of eel and squid. This food was grown on nearby truck farms or fished from the ocean beyond the great harbor. There were household items too, new and used clothing, pots, pans, utensils, all hawked by men who seemed angry that people didn't buy their goods.

Indicating the vendors, Angelina said, "Some are Jews, some are Italians. "The Jews are more honest, but by this much only." She squeezed the tip of one thumb, showing only the end of a red-painted nail. She spoke while steering Mariana around piles of manure and discarded produce, the last picked through by foraging chickens and beggars, some of the latter pointed out by Angelina as being rich men.

In this press of people Mariana locked arms with the aunt for protection as they passed among buildings partly effaced by the brimming overflow of their contents: people on the steps fanning themselves, hanging over rooftops, standing in doorways, sitting in windows as if the last place they wanted to be was inside. There was a tremendous din, a crowd noise that struck like a second wave when they turned onto Canal Street and an even stronger smell of food and sewage. People called from windows and rooftops, peddlers held up their goods and screamed angrily at passersby. They beat on their pots, they waved their dry goods like flags. Chickens and children percolated through all this confusion.

Olga had been right: there were plenty of men on the street. And most of these looked as if their clothes hadn't been changed. Some were dusted with lime, some daubed with tar. L'America was incomprehensibly large and Mariana was only on the edge of it. Here was a place where her past couldn't follow. Looking up and beyond the immediate perimeter of buildings she pointed north and asked Angelina about the people who lived beyond what they could see.

"The Irish," she said, making a chopping motion with the edge of her palm. It was the sign for hitting. Waving a long index finger she said, "You stay here with your own people."

They climbed the steps to a three-story clapboard building. Angelina said something in English to an old man at the door who took a clay pipe from his mouth and laughed, displaying a set of lower teeth rotten at the tops.

"What did you say to him?" asked Mariana.

"*Bus-i-ness*," replied the Aunt, using the English word, and gently pushing Mariana through the door, which creaked loudly. This noise satisfied the aunt, who remarked, "Now we know if they leave without paying."

"Who are you talking about?"

"You'll see soon enough."

Mariana found herself in a hallway lit by an oil lamp. She heard noise from upstairs—doors slamming, pots banging, plates rattling, then heavy footsteps coming down the stairs unevenly.

Angelina placed a protective hand in the small of Mariana's back and told her to hold the pillowcase in front of her. The necessity for her advice soon proved itself.

A man with lime-dusted overalls came toward them, one hand on the bannister, the other on the wall. At the sight of the women he stopped, opened his arms and sang out: "Help me, Angelina! At night I see nothing but men in my room!"

"Protect yourself," said Angelina. "This one has hands like an octopus."

"Please Signorina, I am a gentleman."

"You're a *schifoso*," she said. "Go! *Vatine*!"

Pretending to be hurt, he looked to Mariana for justice. "I have said nothing offensive! This is the truth. I sleep at night with nothing but men. Men over me, men under me, men to the left and right."

Mariana raised her eyes to a handsome young man whose face had assumed a look of comic and falsely threatening intensity. He was lean as a railroad spike, and his arms bulged with hard muscle. His hands were swollen and bruised. His eyes, which maintained their almost insolent stare, were the color of leather.

"My name is Mario," he said. "An Abruzzese." He held on to the bannister and bowed low. "I see you have just arrived in our beautiful L'America. Perhaps we will see more of each other—on an honorable basis, of course. As you already know, I have no woman, and I came to this country for money and a wife. Right now I have neither."

"He's lying about the first," Angelina said. "As for the wife, nobody is certain."

Mario stepped aside gallantly, flattening himself against the wall with his arms outstretched. As they passed by, Angelina said, "Remember, tomorrow is Friday." Her tone of voice was confidential.

"*Signora*," said Mario, "I have lived here for perhaps a century, sleeping like a canned fish next to other fish whose noises, odors, and habits revolt me. Every Friday I have paid the rent. There is no reason why tomorrow should be any different, unless you wish to come and collect it yourself."

"Perhaps I will do that," said Angelina, pushing Mariana forward.

Mariana climbed to the next landing and paused to catch her breath. She looked down and saw Mario and her aunt whispering together. They stopped when they saw she was looking and Mario continued to one of the first floor rooms. Angelina came up the steps and waved her on. "Straight ahead! Straight ahead! We live on the top!"

As the aunt climbed the stairs behind Mariana, she reflected on the similarity between herself and her niece. The two women were fifteen years apart but physically similar. Both were black haired and blue eyed, with their upper front teeth pushing gently on their lips, an evocation of sensuality, but also of death. Both women had become physically mature at an early age, and their longing to love had driven them into the arms of disreputable men.

Angelina's child had been aborted in Palermo. Like Mariana, she'd also done her "penance" in Strufolino's candy factory, and it was a lucky stroke that Mariana began to menstruate when Angelina was still in Sicily. Hoping to avoid repeating the mistake of keeping a woman in ignorance, the aunt had been summoned from Palermo to give Mariana the needed lessons. Until that time Mariana believed that babies popped out of oranges. Later she'd been told an equally incredible story, that babies were expelled from the mouth in a process like forced vomiting.

Angelina's lesson back home with the white stocking was also supposed to explain sex and pregnancy. The aunt now understood that Mariana's memory of her instructions had been selective. At the right time she would take the matter up with the young girl once more to make sure she understood the female cycle. For the immediate future she would give her a diet of hard work.

They climbed to the third floor hallway diffusely lit by a skylight. Mariana made out four doors. One was open to a toilet, the other three were shut, but from behind them emanated the kitchen noises heard from below. Added to these were men's voices, loud and boisterous.

"Who are they?" she asked.

"Don't worry," said Angelina, opening one door to a darkened room with beds and sofas around the perimeter. A cast-iron stove was flanked by a bureau covered with handmade lace and a display of candles, holy pictures, and palm clusters. On a rack above the stove were family photographs, including one of Angelina's marriage to an older man known as Pascuzzo.

"My wedding in Palermo," Angelina said, holding out her arms for more important business: now that they were alone she hugged and kissed Mariana lovingly on the cheeks, then playfully on the lips, pulling at her cheeks with strong fingers for each kiss.

"You're safe now, don't worry. You're safe here with us."

Mariana felt tears trying to come, but they were unable to break through the barrier in her throat. She wanted to ask about her brother and father, but those questions would start a flood of tears. Everything around her except for Angelina and the items reminiscent of home was like the strange and frightful ocean she'd recently crossed. What would she do here? How would she ever learn English? The voices and the clatter she'd heard before were now even closer. They came from the rooms on either side of her: from one, the sound of pots, an organized clinking and banging; from the other, men playing *scopa* and angrily throwing down the cards.

"Don't worry," Angelina said, "I'll explain everything." She pushed aside a heavy curtain that separated the room from a gas-lit kitchen.

The facing wall was stacked with more wine flasks and glasses than any family would need. The stove in this room was hot, and pots of water and tomato sauce simmered on top.

Angelina set down a plate of macaroons and a bottle of Anisette. She pulled the cork with her teeth, poured out two glasses. With the sweet, familiar smell, Mariana relaxed, and immediately began to cry. She pushed the cookies and liquor forward and covered her face. She knew crying would contort her features, and she rubbed herself hard, as if by working the skin she could reverse the process. Her tears fell onto the dress where it stretched over her breasts.

Angelina came behind her and rubbed her neck. "Listen my dear, I know what happened! I know everything! You did what was proper. Now, forget what happened back there and listen to me. I knew that man and all his family. They're first-class animals, first-class! So don't feel bad about what you did. And as for your child—yes I know about that too—consider it a tragedy of life and get it out of your mind. That was another life. Your child is alive somewhere, and with a full belly since they're not given to poor people. When I was in your situation, I wasn't allowed to give birth at all, if you can understand my meaning. Yes dear, I made the same mistake, so don't feel bad. I know how men are!"

"And what does my father think?"

"Your father would never admit it, but he's proud of you. You'll see. He'll show himself as soon as it's safe to come. Then you'll see how much he loves you."

"When will he come?"

"Don't worry, you will like it here and learn much."

Mariana ate the macaroons and drank two small glasses of Anisette, a combination that dulled the anger and frustration with her father. If he was so proud of her, why wasn't he here to greet her?

She looked up to Angelina, who was drying dishes and putting them away. The sight of a confident woman busy with kitchen chores made her feel sleepy and secure for the first time since leaving home. She would have a bed in the main room, where the aunt had arranged some curtains for her privacy.

"Why are you angry with your father?"

Mariana toyed with the macaroon crumbs on her plate, pushing them first one way then the other. A constriction in her throat threatened to open and let out tears. "Because he wasn't here to meet me."

"Tell me, how can you be angry when your father loves you?"

Words broke the constriction in her throat. They tumbled out with her tears. She'd done what was expected, she'd done what was right. He himself had threatened Nicolo on the day he went to L'America. She also told Angelina that her father had killed a boss in the south.

"What boss?"

"One who cheated him of his pay."

"Who told you this?"

"Franco."

"How does he know?"

"People know, that's all."

The aunt wiped Mariana's eyes. The girl was strong and full of energy, like herself at that age, all impulse, all emotion. Ready to believe anything as well. Mariana's father killing a boss? Possible, but not likely. But maybe that was why Santo wouldn't live near Mulberry Bend, where the population was predominantly Sicilian and his past might catch up with him.

"There's something you must know. Your father may pay with his life for what you've done."

"I already know that."

"He lives in danger every day. Did you know the dead man's brother works in this part of the city, not ten minutes from here?"

"And where is my father?"

Gently, Angelina turned Mariana's face up to her own. "Your father needs to provide a home for you and Franco. This is the first thing on his mind. But until this matter is settled, you and Franco will stay with me, here in the boarding house."

"And why can't I know where he lives?"

"Because you can't be seen together."

Angelina drew Mariana close. The young girl felt the soft cushion of her aunt's breasts. There was comfort there, and strength to protect a niece and a brother. She relaxed into Angelina's softness, smelling that mixture of sweat and perfume that reminded her of the women at home. This was her goal for L'America: to have a man's authority, like her aunt. She would need that kind of strength to live here.

CHAPTER 24

To strangers he said, "My name is Santo. You have just arrived in L'America? Then I can be of service. Do you need a room for sleeping? Someone to write a letter? Do you need work? A haircut? A woman? I know someone who can arrange that too, yes, even a woman. Let me tell you something else. Before you buy olive oil or cheese from any of these high-priced *grosserie* or these petty thieves in the streets, ask them the price. Then come to me. You'll see what I can do."

His cover for the past was to live in the open. He was a man of business who kept his name. He bought his goods from sneak thieves, peddlers, large importers, from Italian seamen on the nearby piers. He and Paolo Nerone rented a store on West Thirty-Fourth Street, within sight of the piers for the Italian lines. The area was predominantly Neapolitan, and this worked to Santo's advantage. He needed to keep his distance from Carmelo and the Sicilians downtown.

The business wasn't quite what Paolo had in mind when he'd proposed a partnership. The neighborhood was less transient than the Little Italy of Mulberry Bend. The tenements in the upper Twenties and lower Thirties had more families than single men, and women weren't so easy to find here. Prostitution was tolerated in Palermo, even regulated by the police. In L'America the "regulation" took the costlier form of bribery, and Paolo was hard put to keep more than two women working. As a result he devoted himself increasingly to furthering Santo's conception of the business: a store that operated ostensibly as a bar and cafe, but where the owners sold anything they could get their hands on.

Business was as changeable as the sea. When Italian ships were in port, the poorly furnished restaurant couldn't seat all the seamen. When there were no ships because of dock strikes or schedule breaks, there was no business. A steady income could be had only by selling coffee, cheese, olive oil, household items new and used, even haircuts and shaves, at which Paolo was expert. Most of the food, including ice and coal, was stolen from the railroad cars parked on the streets as part of the New York Central Railroad system. The thieves were the young men of the neighborhood, who stole for their friends and families. When they came upon goods in great quantity, they passed them on to Santo.

The store had no sign or identifying feature. Like many stores in rapidly changing neighborhoods, it had never served one purpose for long. It was a glass-fronted room, elevated from the sidewalk. The room had a few tables and chairs, a cooking stove in one corner, some shelves with dishes, cups, and glassware. A doorway led to a pair of back rooms. The view was blocked by a beaded curtain.

Santo lived in one of the back rooms with his cot squeezed between sacks and barrels. He learned to sleep through boat horns and the screech of rolling steel as railroad cars moved around, but sometimes he was kept awake by the hushed, urgent voices from the room where Paolo's women worked. Their voices and the heavy footsteps of drunks left him even lonelier than he'd been at the boarding house in New Orleans.

Paolo put himself into the business with great fervor. He soon established contacts with seamen as well as importers downtown. He wore vested suits and a derby hat cocked to one side. He also became Santo's trusted friend. He knew what had happened in Castellano, but his knowledge didn't come exclusively from Santo. The two men were cousins with Strufolino. It was Paolo who set up the meeting in Palermo where Mariana observed Nicolo with the prostitute.

Paolo became Santo's ear to the Sicilians in Mulberry Bend. He often went to the *Batteria* to solicit new immigrants. When he did so, he would visit Angelina and bring back the news.

"Guess who I met downtown?" Paolo said to Santo one morning.

Santo was in the front room preparing to shave. In the mirror he saw Paolo draw pensively on his cigar. Worry lines gathered on his forehead. His hat was off, and his bushy hair was uncombed and pushed to one side.

Santo lathered his face, then reached around and took a careful stroke on his left sideburn, keeping the razor steady.

"Your friend, the butcher," said Paolo.

"What did he say?"

"He told me a tale of woe, to which I was sympathetic. His younger brother was found in a tower near Castellano, buried under some stones. The body had been torn apart by wild animals. This was what hurt him most."

"How much do you think he knows?"

"He asked if I knew someone from Castellano named Santo Regina. And when I said I didn't, do you know what he said? That he'd seen me several times go into your sister's boarding house on Elizabeth Street. And when I told him I didn't know whose sister the woman was, he wouldn't believe me. At this point I pretended to cooperate, telling him I'd heard something in the boarding house about a brother who'd gone to Illinois to work on the farms, but I couldn't tell whether my answer satisfied him. He wanted to know where I was working."

"What did you tell him?"

"Another lie. I gave him the names of friends who will support my story."

At the sound of footsteps on the sidewalk, Paolo went to the window, looked through the side of the shade, then motioned that all was safe outside.

"He made me afraid, Santo."

"I would have been afraid myself."

"What do you think will happen?"

"I could walk into the butcher shop and put a bullet into his heart. I could stuff him into a barrel filled with cement and throw him in the river. That's the way The Black Hand does it."

Paolo ran his hands through his hair. He looked down, then away. "You must do something," he said.

Santo wiped his face with a wet cloth. "What can I do?"

"Take your children and leave the city."

"I can't do that?"

"Why not?"

"Because as much as I'm afraid, I can't show it."

Paolo left the room and brought back a chair. He dusted it with a handkerchief and sat down. "I'm going to tell you a story. And when I'm finished, maybe you'll listen to reason. How much do you know about this Carmelo?"

"He's like the others," said Santo. "What else is there to know?"

"I will tell you what else," Paolo said. "Near your town there was a small estate owned by two brothers named Palazzola. These were frugal men who made their money fishing out of Termini. They sold their boat and became farmers because they were that rare kind who love the land more than the sea. They bought land and built a house shared by their families, and they began to raise wheat and livestock. They also had a number of grown children between them, handsome sons and daughters all. They were very efficient farmers, even working the land around their house, where they also kept animals for home use.

"There was however, a boundary dispute with the owner of an adjacent property, one Don Calogero, a man I'm sure you know of, since many Castellanese worked for him. Over the years Don Calogero had asked the former owners of the Palazzola land to sell him the disputed portion, a fraction of a *tumolo* protruding into Don Calogero's vine plantings. The don claimed this land had once belonged to his own family, from which it had been taken by force. But this had happened so many generations ago that nobody knew whether the don was telling the truth.

"The Palazzola brothers were ignorant of this disagreement between Don Calogero and the former landowners. The brothers also didn't know that the land had been sold precisely because the former owners no longer had stomach for the kind of fighting required to keep it. But as a parting blow to their enemy, these men told the Palazzola brothers that this piece of land once formed the core of the original estate. They went so far as to say that the land had been the site of a medieval village, and that holy artifacts were buried there. The Palazzolas thus became attached to the little parcel, and refused every offer from Don Calogero to buy it.

"Don Calogero was a man of great influence. But he couldn't very well go to the local *mafiosi*—men like himself—and enforce a just settlement when he couldn't prove his cause was honorable. So he returned to the tactics proven successful against the former owners. He began to harass the brothers, slowly at first, stealing a few goats or sheep, on one occasion a cow, not hurting the Palazzola shepherds but simply tying them up while taking what he wanted. None of this work was carried out by Don Calogero personally. It was done by his hired group of men posing as bandits. They were always mounted on fine horses that only the wealthy could afford.

"Now the boss of this group was a young man who, at the age of eighteen, was sent to the Ucciardone Prison for stealing mules. He choked a guard to death and escaped, then went to live in the hills of Montelepre with similar types. These men knew how to change the colors or markings on horses and mules and pass them along without suspicion. That young boss was your friend, Carmelo Infante, Nicolo's brother, and known as Carmeluzzo.

"During all this time nothing was said between Don Calogero and the Palazzola brothers. There was never an ultimatum, never a demand. And truly, the first thefts of animals were assumed to be the work of bandits. The peasants who worked for the Palazzolas recognized this Carmeluzzo, something easy to do from a distance because he is so short, and at the same time so heavy that he needed the strongest horse. When mounted, Carmeluzzo resembled an egg with tiny legs. He was greatly feared, and one reason was his expert ability with a Mauser. His tactic on any raid was to shoot an animal close to the shepherd from two or three hundred meters.

"The Palazzola brothers—Gondolpho and Antonio—now patrolled their land with shotguns. One day when the brothers failed to return, their two sons—Paolo and Arcangelo—rode out to search for them. They discovered that all the vines and olive trees in the disputed land had been cut down.

"It was a well chosen time for such destruction, just before harvest, when the vines were heavy with grapes like the beards of men, and the silver begins to show on the olive leaves. Observing no signs of Don Calogero's men, the younger men dismounted and walked through the trampled vines and cut branches, trying to read tracks and footprints.

"They soon came upon Gondolfo tied to one of the standing trees, his face torn away by a *lupara* blast. There was no sign of his brother, Antonio. In these situations, moments of clarity often precede the outlet of emotion. So it was with Paolo and Arcangelo, whose father was tied up and murdered. During those seconds before emotion took root, the boys coldly determined that a small-caliber bullet had entered Gondolfo's head from behind and below the ear, while the point of its exit had been obliterated by the *lupara* blast.

"Arcangelo's cry of outrage for his father's death was simultaneous with a Mauser shot. *Zinga!* Paolo went down and died. The bandits then charged. Arcangelo was taken prisoner and led to a nearby hut, where he found his uncle, Antonio, wounded in the legs but still alive.

"Now the Palazzolas were far from meek. They were unwilling to give up, even with the deaths of their key men. Upon receiving news that Gondolfo and Paolo were dead, and that Arcangelo and Antonio could be ransomed for a sum equal to the value of their estate, the family went to the *carabinieri* in Palermo. A captain there, taken with Gondolfo's widow, promised to hunt Carmeluzzo and his gang to the last man, and he rode into the hills with a contingent of forty men. This captain was named Finelli, and was one of those types who took police work seriously.

"But as always with bandits, after they strike they are nowhere to be found. A network of fear protects them. They return to towns where sympathizers harbor them. Or they resume the peasant life, plodding into the fields alongside their beasts. So Finelli combed the countryside, searching every town and cave and grotto, looking in every face. But no trace of Carmeluzzo or the Palazzolas was found. Finelli spoke in secret to the former owners of the Palazzola estate and with other leaseholders, of course learning nothing. As a last resort he even arrested Don Calogero, riding on to his land with all of his men. The old Don admitted nothing and was soon released. But he was so offended by this invasion that he vowed revenge.

"Finelli's purpose in arresting Don Calogero was not to extract information, but to draw Carmeluzzo into the open. Upon learning what had happened to his patron, the bandit sent Finelli a note, stating that he and his men had merely been resting from their labors. True to their word, the theft of livestock on the Palazzola estate resumed: in each case the shepherds were bound up while Carmeluzzo took what he wanted.

"Finelli now pretended to give up. He sent most of his men back to Palermo. He hoped their obvious movement would be seen by Carmeluzzo as a victory. He and the remaining men then retired to a cave stocked with provisions and which overlooked a path used by the band.

"One day a lookout spotted Carmeluzzo and four men making their way along the path and leading several fine-quality mules. Finelli and his men mounted and gave chase, not surprised when the thieves cut the mules free. Putting their own horses into a dead run, Carmeluzzo and his men disappeared over a hill.

"The *carabinieri* followed at full speed, figuring the bandits' tired horses would soon give out. They came over the hill in a tight group—and this was their mistake—galloping so fast there was no way to avoid the hail of gunfire which greeted them from the bandits waiting just over the crest. Finelli and three others went down in the first volley. The remaining few were slaughtered as they turned and ran.

"This was the last sight of Carmeluzzo in Sicily, and many say that an agreement was struck with the *carabinieri*. Either the bandit left Sicily or they would marshal hundreds to avenge Finelli's death. Thus you see how the government works in collusion with such outlaws. Carmeluzzo was unofficially deported to L'America, where he still serves at the call of gangsters and politicians because he owes them his life.

"As for the Palazzolas, Arcangelo and Antonio were killed and buried with the others. The bodies of all four—fathers and sons together—were found in shallow graves."

After a pause Santo said, "How do you know this story?"

Paolo looked away from Santo for the first time since beginning the story. "Carmeluzzo and his bunch would come to my mother's house in Palermo. The story was passed to the women and back to me. He was the one man my mother feared, friendly one moment, hateful the next. There was no way to predict what would give him offense. Now, tell me, did you know this man was such a beast?"

Santo said, "When I was a boy in Castellano these stories were kept from me, or else I chose not to hear them. Unlike most boys, I didn't believe that bandits were heroes. We assumed that Carmeluzzo stole from the poor as well as the rich. The vicious kind of murder you speak of, we could do nothing about that."

"Now do you see why you must do something?"

"What would you have me do?"

"What do you think?"

"I think he's an old man, and the words he spoke to you today were just that, words."

"Do you know what he said to me? 'Nothing deserves a death, except another death.' Do you think that because he has no horse and Mauser he can't kill a man? Someone like him has others do his bidding. What do you think? How many Italian stores are blown to bits by dynamite after their owners receive letters from the Black Hand. This is just another name for personal vengeance! Do you see all the buildings going up in this city? All the cellar holes blasted through the rock of Manhattan with dynamite? How many Italian workers steal some dynamite from the job and sell it to those who make bombs? Carmeluzzo doesn't have to come near to kill you."

"But I can't simply kill him."

"How can you say that?"

"Very easily. Do you think killing is an art one learns? That done even once, the second time is easier? That done from passion it can be done without passion?"

"You surprise me," said Paolo, rubbing some spittle over a crack in his cigar, then trying to make it draw. As their friendship strengthened, Paolo had become less deferential to Santo. This was a welcome change, but the source of the new attitude wasn't Paolo's maturity. It was the new friends downtown—gangster types who earned their living as thieves, and perhaps as the Black Hand extortionists Paolo seemed to deplore.

"You misjudge me, Paolo. You think I'm capable of murder."

"This is the reputation you carry."

"I never killed that boss down south."

"That may be so, but Carmeluzzo fears you as much as you fear him. You should take advantage of that."

CHAPTER 25

Carmelo Infante knew it would be impossible to lead a life in L'America that resembled the previous one, where he lived with a band of men in caves and huts, or at friends' houses far from the places where he did his work. His first few months in the new country found him without friends. This change was so difficult that for some time he was unable to look for the most menial work. He sat in a basement room on Baxter Street and drank himself to sleep every night. It was only when his money ran out that he found a job in the nearby butcher shop. He eventually bought half interest in this business with money from the sale of land back home.

During his first years in L'America he didn't meet a single Sicilian who'd done business with him in the old days. Later on, however, he was invited by newly arrived friends to take part in whatever illegal business they could drum up. These men had devised numerous schemes to be carried out at the expense of the newly arrived southern Italian. He'd refused without a second thought. A few years in the Italian section had shown him how hard life could be, and he no longer had any sympathy with thieves.

In Sicily his work had evolved from necessity. One bit of trouble led to another until there was no turning back. He'd known nothing else. He didn't remember how it began. There was no first crime leading to a second and a third. There was only this: as a child he was reviled by everyone, including his father, who called him *faccia brutta*: ugly face. He was nearly as short as a midget, with a turned and shortened leg that never corrected itself, even with the applications of herbs and holy water by every priest and healer his mother could find. And whether this deformity had caused people to dislike him, or him to dislike people, was a question he no longer asked. Only his mother had kissed him. His father gave him nothing but the back of his hand.

So he went away. His thievery and killing came as naturally as hair grew. It was a maturation process. One day he killed his first man, a shepherd shot from two hundred meters. The man had been thrown back as if kicked by a mule. Sometimes Carmelo tickled the recollection. He saw the man fall back, his tattered clothing flapping like tiny flags. The Mauser delivered death from a distance. The close work came later, after his imprisonment—the guard he'd choked for example. His desire to become more feared seemed as natural as his present wish to sell more meat. A man's work became a natural part of him.

Now, as a butcher, he earned more money than as a bandit. He lived well. There was no need to look over his shoulder. Occasionally a Sicilian would stare at him with a look of tenuous recognition; occasionally a man would greet him on the street with a slight bow, barely perceptible, and address him as Don Carmelo. He would react to these men with a childlike modesty, for he was still creating a legend, albeit a new one.

He should be content with his new life, but he wanted to go home again. He hated the crowded city with its strange nationalities, its Jews, Orientals, English, its gangs of Irish boys who'd once pelted him with eggs. He didn't like adjusting to different languages, even the other Italian dialects, which would soon obliterate his native speech. He wanted to retire on the family land in Castellano. There was so much of it. He could build a house in the hills where his vines would flourish among the clouds and he could tend them like an angel. This was how he wanted to spend his last years, and why it had been so important for Nicolo to stay home and keep the land.

Shortly after the killing of Finelli and his men, Carmelo went home to say good-bye to his mother and younger brother. Nicolo was fifteen at the time, and was playing outside when Carmelo arrived. Nicolo and some other boys had mounted a donkey and were beating it with sticks to make it move. Being the smallest in the group, and the first to be thrown off, Nicolo's job was to whack the stubborn animal in the rump, and when it started to move, throw himself onto the lap of one of the riders. But when he did this, the older boys pushed him to the ground as a reward for his labors. Carmelo watched this happen several times. Then he called the boy inside.

"Which one is the donkey?" he asked.

Nicolo shrugged. "What do you mean?"

Carmelo took him by the ears and turned his face up. He was a short, well-proportioned boy, with none of the unnatural maturity about his face that Carmelo had exhibited at an early age, and no twisted leg causing men to dislike him instantly.

"Don't you see what's happening out there? Your friends made a donkey out of you!" He released him roughly. The boy needed an older man to teach him. Nicolo went to his mother, who put her arm around him protectively. Carmelo was tempted to take hold of the boy and shake some sense into him.

Now the mother stepped between them. To Nicolo she said, "Come, give your older brother a kiss. He's going to L'America, and who knows when you'll see him again. Carmeluzzo! Don't look like that! He's just a boy! Come now, a kiss between brothers."

Nicolo kissed Carmelo on the cheek and said into his ear, "Take me to L'America."

Ordinarily Carmelo would have welcomed this display of boldness. But the remark was a frustrating reminder that one reason for his visit was to make sure he had something to come back to. He raised his hand to strike the boy. The mother took his hand and held it, a plea for leniency in her look.

"I want to go with you now!" cried Nicolo.

"Take him," said the mother. "I'm tired." She looked at Carmelo with small, withered eyes and a face full of wrinkles. "Take him," she repeated. "He has no life here."

"And the land? This house?"

She shrugged. "We'll sell it."

"Then sell it to me, for I plan to come back here."

He'd brought a coin for Nicolo, a gold *Marengo* worth several hundred lire. Concealing it in his palm, he reached down and pulled Nicolo to him by the trouser pocket, at the same time shoving the coin down inside it.

"There's something in your pocket," he said, as if he'd just felt it. "What is it?"

Nicolo pulled out the coin, impressed by the gold but seeing through the diversion: He still wanted to go to L'America. His eyes were sharp and dark. "Are you going to take me or not?"

"Keep that coin instead. It's worth a great deal."

Nicolo looked at the coin, then dropped it at Carmelo's feet. Carmelo struck him so hard that he went down on his back. "Your place is here, with your mother. And remember, sooner or later I'll come back to see what kind of life you're leading."

Nicolo hadn't taken to that life, even though he'd been left with so much land that the income from rental was enough to support him and a family. Too many men had returned from L'America with money in their pockets and stories of the free way of life. In L'America a man could do whatever he wanted for a living. And it was a place where people minded their own business.

He wrote Carmelo about his desire to come to New York. As soon as their mother died he had no reason to stay home, and he would therefore sell the land and emigrate. Without giving her name, he even mentioned a *fidanzata* who would come with him.

Carmelo replied with a threat: no brother waited in L'America. If he wanted food on his table, he would find it in Castellano. Then he took a chance: he sailed home for a visit, but not to Castellano. He arranged a meeting with his brother and mother at the home of some friends in Altavilla, people with a daughter whose marriage would include a dowry of land. The woman wasn't attractive, but her land would double Nicolo's income. Nicolo seemed content with the arrangement. He made no mention of the woman he'd written about.

While convincing Nicolo to marry this woman, Carmelo painted a picture of L'America so distasteful and inhospitable that Sicily seemed like a paradise. He also promised to pay Nicolo a monthly sum as a lease fee for his portion of the family land. He returned to L'America confident that his years there would be short. He would finish his life among the vines and snows of Castellano.

CHAPTER 26

When Carmelo's mother wrote him of Nicolo's death she said there was trouble with a woman. Her letter arrived nearly simultaneous with immigrants from Castellano who also told Carmelo that a woman was involved. These people didn't hesitate to give their theories. It was a matter of honor. The girl's father, a widower who'd stabbed a boss to death in New Orleans, was not a man to be trifled with. He and Nicolo had disappeared at the same time. The widower was no doubt in L'America because his sister lived in New York City.

Carmelo stood at the cutting block and stared at his mother's letter as if by perusing its feeble script he could wipe away its meaning. It was early evening. The rush of business was over. Angelo Russo, his partner, was now sweeping the day's worth of sawdust and offal into the street. As Carmelo watched Angelo flush away the refuse of his labor, he was reminded that he was stuck in this city with its foreigners and filthy streets, with its gangs of all kinds, with its human vultures. In the month it had taken for his mother's letter to reach him, the old woman could be dead. And knowing the corruption of Sicilian law, the family property could end up in the hands of Nicolo's wife. He could lose his land, even if he did survive or manage to reverse the widower's revenge. Surely he was Santo Regina's next target.

He scraped his butcher board with a piece of steel flexed in his hands, cutting through the day's work to new wood. He felt a tremor in his stomach, then a fearful, angry squeezing in his heart, a hot rush to his face that put pressure behind his eyes. He gave a little laugh before the tears came, noticing that Angelo was discreet enough to work in a distant part of the store whenever Carmelo looked at the letter.

Carmelo untied his apron and went outside for some air. He smelled the prickly odor of burning coal and headed down Canal Street for the river, hoping that a walk would clear his thoughts. Strolling among the carts and peddlers, he reviewed his situation. He'd been wise to keep his land in Sicily because his reputation was dying there. However that reputation had followed him here as criminals sought him out. Here he attracted all types, vicious men unafraid to kill and extort, greenhorns needing partners familiar with the city. But he also attracted the police and the Immigration Bureau, authorities who feared that Italians were importing a crime-ridden way of life that would ruin the country.

The trick, Carmelo reasoned, was to pretend a fear of deportation when in fact it should be his goal, now that Nicolo could no longer manage his land.

Carmelo's challenge was how to deal with that special squad of police, a contingent of men who spoke the southern dialects. They would come to the shop and ask questions about this or that man, and always with the same threat: that if he didn't cooperate, he would be deported. Carmelo pretended to fear their loud and brash threats. These police were naive youngsters who enjoyed their power. During their first visit to the shop they ran their clubs along the cages to scare the birds. They threatened to deport both Carmelo and Angelo. To hear Sicilian dialect issue from American police was like suddenly confronting trained dogs, or human animals bred for the single purpose of intimidating Italians in their own language. And their boss, to whom they were slavishly loyal, was Detective Joseph Petrosino, a hero among the Americans, but something less to those Italians who didn't like his methods. Petrosino was the man to watch.

When first confronted by Petrosino, Carmelo saw a man who resembled himself: a short man with that suffering, angry look that bespoke a lifetime as an outcast. The detective's face was swollen and pallid, the skin marred with pocks and lines said to have come from a childhood disease.

Petrosino made regular visits to the butcher shop. Each time he would mention a fact of Carmelo's life in Sicily. This was an old police trick used to demoralize a man. Even when Petrosino recounted certain crimes in detail, such as the killings on the Palazzola estate, Carmelo held up his hands in a helpless gesture as if his former life of crime was something he could do nothing about. Petrosino never tried to extract anything that Carmelo didn't want to talk about. Carmelo knew the reason for this too: the detective was cultivating him for the day when he would be asked something important. When he would be given a choice: to cooperate or face deportation. Such a threat would play right into his hands.

The visits were beneficial to both men. The detective was eager to defer to the older man's experience, so he always asked for information indirectly. This appealed to something in Carmelo. He and Petrosino would talk in the well-heated back room of the shop where the incubators were kept. Coffee or cold drinks would be brought by a boy from a nearby cafe who looked starry eyed at Petrosino's openly displayed pistol. The detective's presence also gave Carmelo a certain public notoriety that worked to his advantage. The regular police left Carmelo alone, and the neighborhood Italians respected him out of fear, and sometimes admiration. This brought business into the shop.

Carmelo had given the detective a key to the incubator room, which could be entered from the alley. It was clear that Petrosino liked to relax in that room, and Carmelo would often enter in the morning to find the detective asleep on the table with his head resting in his hands. Carmelo would then order coffees for both of them, and Petrosino, thus revived, would talk about the main problem of his job: how American laws allowed criminals to slip from justice once they reached the courts, how lawyers could have them released on fine constitutional points.

"The law in Italy favors the state," said the detective. "That in L'America favors the individual. This is why we need to change things."

Carmelo headed for the Hudson River, hoping the fresher air would suggest a strategy for dealing with Petrosino's veiled threats. In his favor, he sympathized with the detective's complaints about the justice system. He no longer identified with the criminal element, whose main targets were working men like himself and poor immigrants trying to make a living. He'd never harmed or stolen from such people. This was an impossible concept. They had nothing worth stealing, and with Petrosino he sympathized with those who suffered from criminals whose method of intimidation was a bullet or a stick of dynamite.

A group of criminals known as the Giuseppe Morello Gang was Petrosino's running passion. He believed them responsible for the murder in which an Italian was found buried in sawdust inside a barrel. Petrosino knew who did it, but couldn't produce the witnesses. And the city's English and Italian newspapers followed Petrosino at every step of the investigation, a Petrosino for once reluctant to talk to the press.

Several members of the Morello gang had been arrested, but all had been released from jail after their lawyers argued that police procedures violated the rights of the accused.

Giuseppe Morello, however, was an old friend. Back home he and Carmelo had moved stolen animals between Sicily and the mainland. He was a good man, always giving Carmelo the benefit of the doubt in their dealings. There had never been ill will between them. He'd come to L'America several years after Carmelo, and immediately made his visit, at which time Carmelo refused to join him.

Since that time Carmelo had been able to use his influence with Morello to ease the burden for several friends whose businesses had been threatened. One word from Carmelo, and Morello would take their circumstances into account. All this was done without any sign from Morello that he would expect a favor in return. As he said to Carmelo, "We are old friends. And what I do for you requires nothing. You want to have your own life, and this is just as well." With this, the two men had embraced and parted company.

Since the day Morello was arrested for the barrel murder, Carmelo knew Petrosino would come to him. There was too much pressure on the detective to solve the crime. The newspapers were mocking the "Italian Expert," and some were asking whether the cost of this special squad was justified when so many murders and bombings were still unsolved. Petrosino in turn was using the newspapers to complain about the lack of help both from the city and from Italians themselves. He also said in private that another man had ordered the execution of the man in the barrel. That man was Vito Cascio Ferro.

Carmelo had met the notorious Don Vito only once. During his bandit days he'd been approached by an intermediary who said that an unnamed man wanted some mules stolen from an estate. When the man specified that the mules were to be killed, Carmelo reminded him that his custom was to keep any animal he stole for later sale. A meeting was called with Don Vito. This took place in open country, and the don appeared on a donkey laden with freshly cut *sulla*. His face was unshaven, and bunches of the red-flowered legume were tied to his donkey.

Carmelo knew the man's reputation. Don Vito had once been

arrested for kidnapping a baroness in Palermo. He successfully defended himself by claiming he loved the woman and she'd agreed to the elopement. Don Vito had also incited peasant uprisings in the mountain towns of western and central Sicily. He was a wealthy man who leased most of his land free to the peasants near his home. Carmelo smelled a good fee. Here was a rich man who could be taken.

Later Carmelo would know only that he, armed with two pistols, a knife, and his famous Mauser, had agreed to slaughter any animals he took, and to slaughter them according to Don Vito's specifications: leaving the headless carcasses at the door of the man who committed the offense. This meeting had been Carmelo's only exposure to Don Vito's stern magic. There'd been nothing but soft and even speech from the taciturn man, who seemed more imposing even though he sat a smaller animal. And afterward, try as he might, Carmelo couldn't remember one word that passed between them. He only remembered that later he felt sick to his stomach and couldn't eat for days, not because he'd been insulted—Don Vito had been most polite—but because he had met the man he wanted to be.

Petrosino was no match for Don Vito, whose ability to make men work for him was not based on fear. The don could reassure and command simultaneously. He possessed the aura of cold nobility. And while Carmelo was indifferent to the conflict between Morello and Petrosino, he had to keep both at arm's length.

CHAPTER 27

Upon returning from his walk along the river, Carmelo found Petrosino in the incubator room.

"You don't know what a fool they made of me!" said the detective, holding up a newspaper with the story of how Morello and his friends had been released with a warning by the judge against shoddy police work.

Carmelo busied himself with the incubator box, checking the light bulb and the thermometer. He didn't like Petrosino's arrogant assumption that he was at the detective's beck and call. Their "friendship" still had boundaries. Carmelo cleared a space on the table, washed out two glasses, and poured some Fernet in each. At the front of the store he signaled across the street for coffee. After returning he fussed with the incubator a little more, aware that the detective wanted him to sit and listen.

Petrosino now stared at Carmelo from across the table, leaning back and holding up the inky glass of Fernet as if toasting his friend's loyalties.

"What is it?" asked Carmelo, impatient with this presumption in the detective.

"There is that man who is behind all of this," said Petrosino, drinking off part of the Fernet and patting his lips with a handkerchief. "And he is the worst criminal type, since crime to him is a game played for excitement and pleasure. Such men want more than money."

Carmelo looked at Petrosino as if puzzled. He sensed that their friendly relationship was about to become something else. All the quiet afternoons they'd spent together with the common idea rising like steam from their coffee that they were a pair of misfits women wouldn't look at. This mutual bond was coming apart.

"I'm learning even more about you," said Petrosino, finishing his drink and holding up his hand to refuse a second.

"I have much to hide," said Carmelo, smiling and thinking how being deported by this two-face would be welcome.

"There is another man once employed by the one just mentioned. This man stole mules from an estate near Salaparuta, and afterwards he killed them."

"And if I am this other man, so be it."

"You worked for the man I have in mind. You stole for him."

"I know the man you have in mind, but that incident was long ago and back on the other side of the world."

The detective nodded. "Then you can tell me where he is."

"I have heard, in New Orleans."

"No!" roared Petrosino, banging both fists on the table so cups and glasses bounced and the bottle of Fernet fell over. "He is here!" he cried. Rising to his feet, he looked around for something else to beat or kick, and seeing nothing but incubators with the peeping birds he'd alarmed, he began to make queer and frustrated motions with his arms and legs, as though running and hammering in place. He then took the table by its edge and threw it over. Cups and glasses slid to the floor.

Carmelo waited for quiet, then said, "Tell me what you want."

"You must serve me! Not them!"

Carmelo stood back with a bemused look, as an elder might regard a petulant child. He picked up the Fernet and checked for cracks in the bottle. Turning to Petrosino he said, "Bandits or Black Hand or whatever name you use, I'm out of that world. It would be impossible for me to get back in."

"No, Carmeluzzo! This is where you're mistaken! You're getting back in!"

"How?"

"I will tell you soon enough."

After Petrosino left, Carmelo fed some canary seed to some fancy pigeons he kept in a cage. The seed had a high concentration of hemp, which made the birds coo pleasantly. The hens sang clear and sweet, the cocks warbled and brushed the cage bottoms with their spread tails as they strutted. The world was simple again. Carmelo went into the back room, closed the skylight, and decided to drink while he listened to his music.

He poured some wine from a clay jug. The jug had a tiny hole at the top that resisted the flow. The wine fell into the glass with a hollow, musical sound, almost like the ringing of a single chime, reminding him of the best parts of home. He drank the first glass in one gulp to test the quality. He sipped the second. It was good, tawny wine, made with a high concentration of white grapes. It was as strong as the wines from home, and usually taken with lemon-flavored *gazzosa*, especially on hot days.

Lifting his glass, he toasted Nicolo into whatever place the boy deserved, heaven or hell. His mother was still alive back there, the only family member left, and when she died he would drink for her. The strong wine turned him to thoughts he couldn't control. The last time he drank himself to dizziness was when a certain woman went out of his life, not by her choice as by his coming to L'America. That loss had been like a death. Now he would drink for her too, and after a brief cry he would accept his mother's future death and Nicolo's transfer into another world. Then he would decide what to do about these things.

Who was Santo Regina? He didn't know or didn't remember. The last possibility made him finish the third glass of wine and pour a fourth. He hoped that along with tears for Nicolo's death, the wine would help him recall the man who'd killed his younger brother. He was a widower who didn't live in Castellano proper, but just outside it, on the road to the lower valley. Carmelo pictured the house through a fog, and whether it was a real fog like those that sometimes enveloped Castellano, or whether it was a fog in his brain, he couldn't tell.

The wine had worked too quickly. He couldn't focus on a single idea. Nicolo had violated Regina's daughter, that was certain, but with her consent? That was the question. Was there a child? A child of his blood? That was another question, but there were ways of hiding a child, of getting rid of a child. What could he do about all this when there was Petrosino to contend with. Petrosino! That hothead detective who couldn't see past his nose.

Petrosino had turned on him. And why not? In all the months of their "friendship," Carmelo had given him nothing. He'd told him what any Sicilian in the street would know. And what had the detective revealed to him? Plenty: his distrust of the police commissioner, who feared giving an Italian too much power; his dealings with the governor, and even with the President of the United States, who'd been assassinated after the detective's warnings to the Secret Service had been ignored. There was a bloated self-importance in all this. As if the fate of the United States rested with Petrosino and his "Italian Squad."

Luckily, the detective was under the impression that Carmelo feared deportation. Carmelo planted the idea by telling Petrosino what a wonderful life he had in L'America. He intimated that a veritable army of brothers and sons waited in Sicily to kill him. He had Petrosino right where he wanted him, and with this thought, Carmelo rested his head in his folded arms and fell asleep.

CHAPTER 28

Mariana's world was the boarding house and bakery on Elizabeth Street. Here bread was baked twice a day and a steady stream of boarders flowed in and out. She spent most of her time in the upstairs flat, where life and business came together. Bedding and flour sacks took up the living room, and sometimes the flour sacks had to be slept on. When not mixing dough for Angelina's husband, Pascuzzo, she washed dishes or prepared food for the boarders, who ate in the *magazzino*, a room strictly off limits and into which she took every opportunity to peek.

She awoke each morning to the hum of the dough mixer. A weak light shone in patterned squares on the kitchen cabinets, which were empty of their glassware and dishes: these were piled in the sink. Unwashed pots sat on the cook stove, their sides caked with hardened sauce or starch from cooked spaghetti. She would often hear Angelina's voice: "Work! This isn't Italy, where we can sit in the sun and dream."

Life was work and the accumulation of coins. Bread dough was formed into loaves and baked in a brick oven fired with scrap wood. In the morning Franco and Pascuzzo loaded the freshly baked loaves onto the horse-drawn cart and set off through the streets. The bread was sold before noon, after which there was just time enough to eat something and fire the oven for an afternoon baking.

One night the aunt shook her awake. "Your father is in the *magazzino*! Come, he's waiting for you."

"I don't want to see him," Mariana said. She turned over and buried her face under the pillow.

"You can't refuse him."

"I won't see him."

"What should I tell him then?"

"Nothing."

Angelina left the room. When nothing happened for several minutes, Mariana sat up. The room beyond her curtains was dark except for the dying glow of a votive candle on the coal stove. She heard a halting, muffled voice, her father's, it was different now, deeper and stronger. She burrowed back into the bedding. She heard footsteps, then the screech of the curtain being swung aside. She smelled cigar smoke and the wool of his clothing.

"Sit up and look at me."

A lump of anger hardened inside her. She gave birth to this anger as she'd given birth to the child she'd lost because of her own gullibility. The child she should have carried to Nicolo's house and set on his doorstep. The lump was part of her stomach, like the child.

"You don't want to look at me?" Santo asked.

She didn't move. She waited for the words. The praise, the apology. *He was a beast and you did what was proper. I forgive you. I love you. I respect you.* She heard his breathing. The words didn't come and he left the room.

The next day she went downstairs to fetch water. She swung the empty bucket confidently. Santo was waiting in a doorway across the street. He was clean shaven, no greenhorn mustaches for him! The expression on his face was almost a smile. He beckoned her, but she turned into the alley and filled the bucket, not looking to either side, wanting to be the water in that bucket, colorless and cold. She carried the bucket back to the house, looking at the ground.

Angelina was there. "Why didn't you go over to him?"

"Because I didn't want to."

"You were ashamed."

"Yes, I was ashamed. Wouldn't you be ashamed?"

"That was a mistake," the aunt said. "He might not give you another chance."

Pascuzzo, the uncle, knew what had happened back home and had been opposed to taking in Santo's children. He was a quiet man who worried the stub of a cigar in his mouth all day, a stub sometimes lost under his thick mustaches. Angelina sometimes ridiculed his country dialect, especially when they argued, which was always over matters of domestic economy: the use of coal or wood; whether the day old bread was good enough to serve the boarders; and most of all, the strength and quality of the wine Pascuzzo supplied.

It was the uncle's custom to water the wine before daybreak, the hour when Franco was baking bread and Mariana was still asleep. She often awoke to the clink of tin and glass and the cyclical sound of liquid being poured into the wine bottles. She would observe her uncle with the ashen dot of a cigar nestled into his mustaches. With every watered bottle of wine he exhaled a breath of satisfaction. His complete sense of himself drew her to him. This man was happy with his repetitions: his loaves of bread, his measures of water and wine, his consumption of leftover food. Mariana saw him clearly. He lived as he'd been taught, cautiously.

One morning Mariana couldn't sleep and helped him water the wine.

"There!" she said, setting down the last bottle. "If I can't sleep, at least I can work."

Pascuzzo was pleased. He saw that both Mariana and Franco were good workers. He was sorry for the young girl and saw in her willingness to work a hope for change. Anyone who couldn't sleep after a day's work was miserable indeed. Mariana was a truly restless child. He admired her spirit and was touched by the pain she bore, written into her frightened look and the purplish color under her eyes from lack of sleep.

Pascuzzo couldn't express these feelings with words. Instead, on those mornings when she helped him, he invited her to eat. His breakfast consisted invariably of potatoes and eggs, a ritual as regular for him as that of mixing the wine. He cut several leftover potatoes into chunks, fried these in oil until they were crisp and brown, then dropped in three eggs, swirling the mixture so the yolks still remained separate from the whites. He took the pan off the heat when the eggs were barely congealed. They would grow hard in the pan. He would eat these for breakfast and lunch, when he would hollow out some bread and fill it with this tasty, oily mixture. Potatoes and eggs were more special to Pascuzzo than anything Angelina could cook, and a dish he rarely shared.

With the potatoes and eggs before her, Mariana attacked. Her fork struck each morsel from above, then returned to her mouth with a quick snap. She chewed so hard that a muted clicking of her teeth was heard.

"You eat like your father," said Pascuzzo, who'd shared a meal with Santo on the night of the visit.

The remark was meant to put her at ease, but it had the opposite effect. Mariana's fork stopped. A glistening chunk of egg and potato was impaled on its end. Pointing the fork at Pascuzzo, she said, "*You* are my father."

He laughed and said, "I have enough trouble. Do you want to give me more?"

"I won't be a problem," she answered, but she wondered whether to take his remark as a rejection, an insult. She decided to be completely open.

"I have no father. I need a new one, and I'm choosing you."

"Who says you have no father? Your father?"

"I'm sure he did."

"Your father would never say that."

"But he thinks it."

"He's your father, not me."

He looked at her as if seeing through her. She began to eat listlessly as his rejection set in. He was cold and simple, unable to recognize his open cruelty in rejecting her. Let Angelina give him horns. Like her father, he would also feel the withdrawal of her affection. And one day he'd be sorry that she was gone from his life.

CHAPTER 29

Mariana often went shopping with Angelina to Mulberry Bend, an outing in which the two women locked arms and never separated, even when Angelina bargained with peddlers. The outside world presented Mariana with the incongruous sight of Italian peasants uprooted from their natural setting. The same women who carried their burdens on silent country roads now appeared against a background of crowded tenements and streets choked with the goods of commerce. The chaotic world made her restless and afraid.

She took daytime naps in a small vestibule with blankets on the window to keep out light and sound. Even here she found it hard to sleep and sometimes she would remove the window blanket and look out over an alleyway and an empty lot littered with garbage. In the center was a shack with a rusting iron roof, a meeting place for a group of neighborhood boys who smoked, fought, and stole, boys referred to as the *genga*. The shack was not only a home for some of these boys but also a depository for stolen goods—hauled there on baby carriage frames to which wooden crates had been bolted.

The boys were loud and violent, and one day they tied a boy up, stripped off his pants, and beat him with belts until blood ran down his legs. When finished they returned his pants, and from then on he was a member of the gang.

Their leader, named Gennaro, was easy to spot by his curly blond hair and Nordic complexion. He was small and extremely muscular. His body tapered from shoulder to waist. His arms and forearms were as thick as a man's. He had a small, fish like mouth with square, spaced teeth, and an apelike way of swinging his torso from side to side when he walked.

From her window Mariana could see his oversized hands. He was a swaggering, physical boy, a mauler, constantly punching and wrestling to maintain his superiority over the others. His favorite game was one in which he and an opponent took turns punching each other on the arm, each flexing to withstand the shock of the other's blow. These matches would last until one contestant gave up, at which time each would display the red marks on his arm.

Gennaro often looked up at Mariana. She would remain immobile until he looked away. He soon began to wave and call to her. "*Bellezza! Scendi!*" Beautiful! Come down! And if his friends were there when he called her, they would place their hands between their legs obscenely; and Gennaro, as a way of protecting Mariana, would fight with them until they stopped. Confronted with this pack of apes, Mariana would cover up the window and go about her business, convinced of the stupidity of men and reminded of Nicolo and the way men loved to display themselves.

There were periods when she missed her old town, remembering the pleasant days, spreading laundry on the bushes to dry, taking part in the holy feast, eating nuts and cactus fruits in the fall. At times she even thought it possible to live in Castellano again, to live openly with her past. She could do this as a holy figure, a woman more powerful and mysterious than a local nun called Maria Chiara, one who would give advice to troubled souls. Mariana would live alone and have a secret lover. She would support herself with the offerings people gave for her advice. She would be like her grandfather, a man with healing powers who'd seen the ghost of the great Saint, Gangiuseppe.

She would walk proudly through the streets, shrouded and protected by the mystery that someone, perhaps even herself, had committed murder for her honor. Women from all over Sicily would come and ask how to get their men, or how to end the torment of temptation. She would tell them what to do, and how to test their lovers. Even the famous Maria Chiara would make night visits to her house and reveal her burning lusts. She would advise her to exercise those appetites, for only by intimate knowledge of sin and pain could anyone become truly holy.

She was unable to express these feelings of loneliness and nostalgia to anyone. Franco was caught up in work and the extra measure of freedom given to males. Pascuzzo wasn't the least bit nostalgic for home. And if he did refer to "the other side," as Italy was called, it was with a bitter chuckle, as if he'd gotten the last laugh by escaping. Angelina was now her authority figure. Mariana was never to leave the house alone. There would be no school, no friends, no other world but the house on Elizabeth Street.

Mariana saw yet another side to Angelina: the businesswoman. A stranger would enter the boarding house, weary, lonely, desperate for home. Before this man came within earshot, Angelina would say to her cronies, "Who is this *cafone* from the mountains?" And while they chuckled, she would greet the newcomer like an old friend. "Make yourself comfortable! Here you will eat well but pay little. Where are you from? Whatever the town, we know it well. We have cousins everywhere! Now, what can we sell you today? Let's see what you've got down there."

Angelina would then fish through this fellow's shirt and jacket pockets. Finding nothing, she would pat his trousers and come up with a bill. If not, she made certain he didn't want credit.

It was obvious that Mario was her favorite. He often followed her into the kitchen when she was locking up for the night. There they would enjoy a final glass of wine or a cup of coffee and speak in low, guarded tones.

One day Mariana came upon the two of them in the hallway. They parted from an embrace at the sound of her appearance, and Angelina's face froze with a look of anger directed at Mario. Red-faced and swaying drunkenly, Mario was trying to smile at Angelina to keep his composure. At a signal from Angelina he went down the stairs, arrogantly waving good-bye without turning around. When he was out of sight, Angelina turned to Mariana, taking the tray the girl was carrying and setting it down.

"What did you see?"

"Nothing,"

"Listen to me," she said, putting her arm around the girl and looking down into her face so intently and directly that her earrings shook. "I know you're watching me, but what you see between me and these men is only for the sake of business." She waved in Mario's direction as if to dismiss him. "How many men would come to this place if the boss were a man? What you see is something normal among all men, something you should understand. These men have too much to drink, they think of their wives back home and get the usual ideas. Remember, there are many places like ours in this neighborhood, places where men can sleep and eat. But this is the only one where a man can be served by a woman, and that is why we survive. Now, do you understand?"

CHAPTER 30

Heat devils from the bread oven rose from the bulkhead in shapes as elusive as Santo's life. The angry voices of peddlers moving onto the street expressed not only their prices, but their frustration. Some remained in one spot, others kept moving, unable to bear a moment without a sale. Soon the women would come down from the tenements to shop, or haggle from the windows.

Santo waited in a doorway across the street and observed this regularity of life with bitterness. A peddler's fate was also his own, to offer something for a price, but no lower. To Mariana he offered love and his responsibility as a father and family head. She simply needed to apologize, to say, "*Yes Father, I disobeyed you; yes Father, I was foolish; yes Father, I respect you. Yes, Father, I shouldn't have killed him.*"

He'd planned to arrive in L'America, retrieve his children, and restore their names. But the plan hadn't worked. New York wasn't so anonymous as it appeared. Italians were packed into small sections of Lower Manhattan, but many Sicilians from his district knew that Santo Regina had killed not only his daughter's lover, but a dishonest boss in New Orleans. Even total strangers had approached Angelina with whispered congratulations for what Santo had done, or consolation for his impending doom.

An even more absurd aspect of Santo's plan was his dream of marriage to a woman who would complete their home. His only possibility had been Vaccarella's sister-in-law, but when she learned of the two murders he'd "committed," she wanted nothing to do with him.

With a click of shod hooves on cobblestone, Franco appeared in the bread cart, skillfully threading his way through the crowded street. This was Santo's reason for being here, the son who respected him, not the daughter who defied him. Let her come out of the house and try to speak to him. His words were ready: "*Who are you? My daughter? What daughter? I have no daughter.*" He had only a son. Pascuzzo let Franco drive alone now, and the boy scanned both sides of the street, a sign of wariness filling Santo with so much pride that he felt a lump in his throat. Franco drew up and set the brake, noticing his father in the doorway but acknowledging nothing. He came across the street only when Santo signaled.

He pulled Franco into the doorway and kissed him briefly, then stood him some distance away, feeling his arms and shoulders, looking at him for the family signs. Their separation had coincided with Franco's maturing. The boy had filled out. His hands were large. Like those of his grandparents on both sides, they had long, thick fingers. He'd grown taller too, and his face, always slightly drawn, had widened at the cheekbones. His dark eyes had gone from boyish innocence to something serious, even worried. He was bursting to be a man.

"You're not supposed to be here," Franco said. "Somebody will see us together."

"Who will see us?" he teased. "The butcher?"

"Or his friends, you never know."

"I can't hide forever. I need to see my son. I need to hold the family together as best I can." He partly drew the boy close, then looked around at the crowded street. There were so many eyes.

Franco gestured to show that he understood this reluctance to show affection. He too reached partway toward his father, then withdrew his hand. He suddenly smiled playfully. "When can we live together? And what about your wife? What about a mother for us."

"Who told you about a wife?"

"Angelina."

"Your aunt exaggerates. There's no woman just now. Maybe when this trouble is over."

"For how long will we be in this trouble?"

"I don't know. Tell me your name."

"Frank Savino."

"The real one."

"Regina, Franco."

He'd no sooner patted the boy's shoulder and sent him away when he saw Mariana heading for the alley with her water bucket. She looked at him briefly. An impulse moved him to make a sign, to raise his hand, to smile, but another impulse cut it off. She continued on her way. He put the cigar in his mouth and watched her through the smoke. A brightly colored handkerchief was tied around her head, color for the new life she might not share with him.

On the way back to the house she stopped, and on the pretense of switching the bucket from one hand to the other, she faced him. Her look was imploring and furtive. They stared at each other for a moment, each waiting for the other to give a sign. Santo shook his head. He wasn't ready to take the first step.

"And why not?" asked his sister, who'd watched this little scene from upstairs. Angelina came down and they went to a nearby cafe, where she tried to convince him to take Mariana back.

"What did she do? Tell me, what did she do?"

"You know what she did."

"And so what? She shot that son of a dog to please you. And in return you refuse to acknowledge her. Why make her suffer even more?"

"How do you know she suffers?"

"Because I live with her." She leaned forward aggressively. With her prominent nose she looked like the statue on the prow of a ship. It was no wonder to Santo that she attracted men, especially the younger ones, who saw a potent symbol of womanhood. He felt sorry for Pascuzzo.

"Think before you answer," she said. "Do you want her back? Do you want her in your house?"

"I have no house. I live in back of a store."

"And your children couldn't live with you? In the way Italians are stuffed into these buildings like so many sardines you mean to tell me that your children can't live with you, or even visit you?" She rolled her eyes in frustration and stirred sugar into her cup, thinking of a way to explain some basic facts to her brother. She looked at him skeptically. The great difference between them was that he still believed in absolute obedience.

She waved an index finger with a long painted nail. The finger was her instrument of instruction, something she waved or wiggled, or passed before her lips to indicate silence.

"Do you want your daughter back? Then ask her to forgive you. Tell her you're a man who makes mistakes like everyone else. Then see what happens." The index finger came down and she put the coffee cup to her lips.

"She should forgive me? For what?"

"For not trusting her."

"I trusted her once already."

"Then do it again." She rested her hand on his hand and looked at him directly. "Our father used to say that if you wanted to make something of yourself, then do exactly the opposite of what the Castellanese would do. Those were his last words to me before I came to L'America. I'm sure you heard them too. But sometimes I think you've forgotten this advice. Would anyone at home forgive this child? Not even the priests. This should tell you what to do."

CHAPTER 31

The butcher shop smelled of blood and offal and Santo saw his breath as he passed among poultry cages and carcasses of lambs hung upside down. He perused trays brimming with tripes and sweetbreads, livers and kidneys, hearts and brains. He lowered his eyes to the sawdust on his shoes, then straightened up, holding himself high, chafing from the pistol strapped under his arm. For protection only. He'd passed the shop several times, working up the nerve to go inside. He remembered the trepidation felt back home when he confronted Giuseppe Cassino about workers' rights. Now he felt the same way, ready to gamble. His father would have done this, his father who saw the holy monk and who wouldn't take the sulfur miner's ham and sausage. Now he was here to see if this Carmeluzzo was the kind of man to whom he could say, "Listen, your brother is dead, but he left something behind, a child somewhere back there, in someone else's home instead of yours and mine. He promised himself to my only daughter, then married another. Now, tell me, would you have done the same or not?"

Santo approached the counter, a spectator to the exchange between the two butchers and their customers, their remarks punctuated by the pounding of cleavers. The tall butcher in a black watch cap and plaid wool jacket would be Angelo Russo. The short one was Carmeluzzo, a short man wearing a bloodstained fedora with a narrow brim. Locks of sweat-moistened gray hair curled up around his ears and on the back of his neck.

He looked up expectantly. "What do you want?"

Santo pointed to a chicken in one of the cages.

Carmelo fed a wire bent into a U-shape at one end and hooked the unsuspecting bird around the ankle. He pulled it out, cut its throat, then held it over a bucket while it convulsed and bled. All the while he looked at Santo with a quiet curiosity.

"You've been here before," he said.

"Never," said Santo.

He gave the chicken to Angelo in the far corner of the store where it was dipped, plucked, singed under a flame, and then gutted. While this was being done Carmelo busied himself with other work.

The chicken was brought back with its organs on the side. Carmelo picked up his cleaver.

"In pieces," said Santo.

Carmelo brought the cleaver down several times and piled up the parts, slapping the organs on top. Then he took a small knife and held it to the gizzard. Just before slitting it open, he turned to Santo and said, "I'm sure you've been here."

"Why are you so sure?"

"Because I have a good memory."

"I've never been in this store."

"Perhaps, but I've seen you pass by. You look in here like you want something."

"Maybe I did pass by a few times."

"You're Sicilian," said Carmelo. "And judging by your accent, from my part of the country."

"What part of the country is that?"

Without averting his eyes, Carmelo scraped the gizzard clean with one finger. "You know as well as I know. The mountains near Castellano." He rinsed the gizzard in water, breaking eye contact for the first time.

"I'm from near there," said Santo. "Deep in the country."

Carmelo stared at Santo, then shot a warning look at Angelo, who looked up from his work and said, "He doesn't look like a Sicilian. He dresses too well."

Carmelo looked at Santo and smiled. His upper lip seemed to disappear. "What does he know?" he said, referring to Angelo. "He's *napolitano*."

"I know plenty," said Russo, wiping his hands and pulling a newspaper up from under the table. "They're going to deport all you Sicilians for being Black Hand. And do you know who's going to do it? Our friend, the famous detective."

"*Prezzemolo*," said Carmelo, using the Italian word for parsley, which had become Petrosino's nickname.

"You!" said Angelo to Santo. "Do you know this *Prezzemolo*?" He didn't wait for an answer. "He comes in here all the time. Do you know why? Because he thinks that Carmelo here knows who killed the man in the barrel. Do you know about the man in the barrel?"

"Everybody knows about the man in the barrel," said Santo. "It's an old story." He found that Angelo's humor relieved him, and that somehow the worst part of this visit was over.

"But *Prezzemolo* knows who killed him."

"He knows who steals from the Poor Box too," said Carmelo.

"Cascio Ferro killed the man in the barrel," said Angelo. "Every Italian on Mulberry Street knows that."

"*Don Vito* Cascio Ferro," said Carmelo to Santo pointedly. "We must not forget the Don in his name. Do you know him?"

"No," said Santo.

"*Don Vito*," repeated Angelo. "Remember to have respect."

"You're right," said Carmelo. "We must have respect. Tell me," he asked, now pointing to the newspaper in Santo's pocket. "I see you can read the newspaper. What do you think about this Petrosino who wants to deport all Sicilians?"

"He wants to deport *him*," said Angelo, indicating Carmelo, who was holding up the gizzard and scraping the last particles of sand with his fingernail. "Here's a man ten years in this country, nine behind the same counter. Suddenly he's a criminal! You'd better watch it. If Petrosino sees you in here, he'll think you stuffed the man in the barrel just because you're Sicilian. Then you go on the list."

"What list?"

"The list of people to be sent back. Tell me, how long have you been in this country?"

"Too long."

"Good luck," said Angelo, turning his attention to a new customer who'd come up to the counter. Carmelo wrapped the chicken in newspaper and passed it over to Santo. In an intimate tone of voice he asked, "L'America, how do you find it?"

"It's better than home."

"You don't want to go back?"

"Never."

Carmelo tipped his hat back and said, "Why not?" His look was intense, aggressive, and had nothing to do with his question. He came out from behind the counter and accompanied Santo partway to the door. He had time to say, "You didn't come here to buy a chicken," when Angelo's voice boomed from behind them, "Signore *Di-tekka-tiva!*"

Santo looked up and saw Petrosino coming at them. He put his head down and headed for the door.

"Stop!" cried Petrosino. "You! Where are you going? Where have I seen you before?"

Santo heard Angelo say, "He does this to everybody." Heartened by this, Santo turned and looked evenly at the detective.

"Perhaps you've seen me before," said Santo as if slightly offended. "But I don't remember you. Why do you call to me and raise your voice this way?"

"Because he is a detective of the New York City police!" said Angelo, enjoying the game about to be played. In a serious tone he now said, "This is the famous and respected Giuseppe Petrosino, defender of the Italian immigrant!"

Petrosino glanced angrily at Angelo, then turned to Santo. He drew aside his jacket to show his pistol. He was heavier since Santo had seen him in New Orleans. He seemed stuffed into his black suit. His head, with a black derby hat, seemed set on his shoulders like a ball, without the stabilizing benefit of a neck.

"This one claims to be a Sicilian," said Angelo of Santo. "But to tell you the truth, he looks *napolitano* to me, or maybe even a *genoese*. He dresses very well, look at the shoes! Arrest him anyway! Deport him instead of my partner. He is, without a doubt, Black Hand!"

"I know this face," said Petrosino, coming closer to Santo. He held an accusative finger before him as if testing the wind. "I've seen you somewhere," he said. "What is your name?" His false politeness indicated that he might know the answer already.

"Savino, Salvatore Savino."

With a wink of his eye, which implied some conspiracy Santo didn't understand, Petrosino waved his finger and said, "No, it was someone else. Someone who resembles you. You may go."

As Santo turned to leave, he saw Carmelo staring at him coldly.

CHAPTER 32

Holding two empty buckets, Mariana stood before Gennaro, who was leaning against the wall in the alley. His cheeks were lean, his beard stubble thick, his eyes blue around the edges of the pupils; but the middle circle was washed out, a puzzle, but also a space for her to travel. At the sight of his arms she drew breath. They were muscular and long in proportion to his size and covered with soft golden hairs. She wondered what kind of children they would produce together.

"I thought you weren't allowed in the street," he said.

"I can get out if I want."

His look was mocking, but also intense and affectionate.

Not wishing to give him an advantage, Mariana asked, "Where are all your friends?"

"I quit them." He took her free arm and twisted, not to hurt her but to emphasize. Looking down, she saw the tendons move along his forearm like wires. She wanted to rest her cheek there and feel that movement. She wanted the security of that arm around her. She looked hard into his eyes and was lost.

"Have you seen me with them?" he asked.

She looked around, not wishing to answer the question just yet. Farther up the alley a group of women with aprons over their dresses gathered around the water spigot. Some had recognized her as Angelina's niece. At that moment being seen was more worrisome than Gennaro's truth or his lying. She hadn't been given permission to come downstairs. She moved closer to Gennaro. "I haven't seen you with them. But that doesn't mean you quit."

"Feel!" he said, guiding her hand to his heart.

She pressed her palm against his sweater and felt for the heartbeat. She was aware of a double movement, the acceleration of his breath, and the faster, deeper rhythm of his heart against her palm, as if the heart were outside his body. She compared his intense intimacy with that of Nicolo, who was cold as ice. She looked at him until her eyes drew him in. She still tried to read his eyes for the truth. Yes, she no longer saw him with the gang, but this could have been a trick.

"I need more proof," she said.

He pushed her hand away and looked at her with anger and disbelief. She returned the look, fixing him, finding she had to control her urge to tell him what she'd done before in her life. He was also more unpredictable than Nicolo, and this was because they were in L'America. Behavior was more explosive. She was afraid because he knew L'America. A man like him was certain to have other possibilities, other women like herself. Another bout of loneliness would be impossible to bear if she lost him.

"Don't pretend with me," she said, reaching into her apron and showing him a roll of bills in her fist.

"Where did you get that."

"From my aunt's purse."

He reached for the money but she held it away from him. For a few moments they stared at each other, one question in their eyes: could they trust each other?

Mariana looked around furtively. The women near the spigot were watching them. To spite them she took Gennaro's hand and began to bring it to her breast, as a way of reciprocating his earlier gesture. But before he could touch her, she pushed it away.

"What do you think now?" she asked.

"Where and when?" he replied.

The women had drawn their water and came toward them. Mariana picked up her buckets and walked toward the spigot. When she passed the women one of them said something Mariana couldn't hear. Mariana knew them, and they were no friends of Angelina either. One had a husband who drank every day in the *magazzino*. This was the one who made the remark.

"What did you say?" Mariana challenged her.

They kept walking. The woman closest to Mariana turned her head but said nothing. Mariana continued to the spigot, glad that Gennaro witnessed her strong behavior. Now he would respect her. Water poured into one of her buckets with a hollow sound. She said to herself, "If he follows me here, he's mine."

Filling both pails, she watched bubbles form and break in the turbulent water. He was behind her now. She felt his knee on the back of her leg.

"Tell me what you want," he said.

She looked up to the boarding house. The kitchen and living room windows looked out over that part of the alley. The curtains were undisturbed. Then she looked farther up the alley to the metal shack used by Gennaro's gang. None of his friends were there.

"Didn't you believe me?" he asked.

"This is what I believe. You find a job, then get a place to live, perhaps a room. It must be a secret place, far from here, and far from my father. Then I'll come to you."

"Will you marry me?"

"Not yet." She gave him the money. "This is for the room and don't betray me or I'll find you and stick a knife in your heart." She picked up the buckets and headed back toward the street. She climbed the boarding house steps slowly, resting on each landing. After swinging each pail into the kitchen, she saw something that made her feel as if the bottom had fallen out of her stomach.

Angelina was leaning against a cupboard. Her dark eyebrows were furrowed and her earrings trembled. She dangled the empty purse before her.

CHAPTER 33

From inside the store, Santo pushed aside the curtain and looked into the street. A dead horse lay in the gutter. It had been dying for days, its death hastened by some neighborhood boys who'd thrown rocks at the poor beast and then jumped on its belly to release its gas. A police wagon had passed by and done nothing. It was probably a rented horse, worked to death and abandoned. It appeared in the street at the same time as a pile of empty produce crates. These were gone, scavenged for fuel by the same boys who'd tormented the horse. Today the poor animal was beginning to stink, and rats were eating into its eyes.

He dressed and went outside. Winter had blown the streets empty. There was no business. Dock strikes in Naples and Genoa had idled the piers. His supply of goods was cut off. Ranks of freight wagons stood empty on the riverfront. The railroad cars that shuttled to the downtown station were parked, serving as playhouses for the neighborhood children or sleeping places for transients. The air was cold as brass, the everyday neighborhood bustle reduced to singular events—the clatter and creak of a cart, shod hooves on cobblestones, the rough music of swinging chains. This new inactivity brought fears that L'America would fail him, that the great immigration was a bubble that would burst, sending many Italians back home. What would he do then?

When the idleness became unbearable he went back to the store and fell into a fitful sleep. He saw rats eating their way into the dead horse, but he wasn't sure whether he was looking through the window of the store or the window of his mind. Then something shook him awake. He opened his eyes to Paolo Nerone's bucktoothed face.

"Get up! Carmelo's gone back to Sicily! Some friends who arrived today saw him in Palermo, but they think he'll come back here."

"What makes them say that?"

"You think he has no enemies over there? A hundred people want to kill him. He'll come back here, believe me. He'll find out that you killed his brother and then come looking for you."

"There's nothing I can do about that."

"You could explain."

"What, that my daughter did it? Would it matter?"

"One can never tell. He's been working here for so long, it's clear he no longer wants his former life. He's too old anyway."

Santo followed Paolo into the front of the store where they sat down for coffee. He counted out forty dollars and pushed it across the table.

"This is for your half of the business," he said. "This place can't support two of us, and unless the docks open up again, I'll be out of business too."

Paolo pushed the money back and said, "You have worries enough." His movements were clumsy and drunken. Santo looked at Paolo sternly, then passed back the money and held it there. "Take it," he said, rolling up the bills with a quick motion and stuffing them into Paolo's lapel pocket.

Paolo looked down into his coffee and said, "They call me Black Willie now. I have what is called a nickname."

"Congratulations, you're an American."

Paolo blushed. He was still a timid boy wanting life both ways. He could be as ruthless as a gangster and as gentle as a saint. He'd gone back to wearing the clothes in which he'd arrived in L'America, the mouse-colored suit, the black sweater with its moth eaten front. He was working downtown now, but was never specific about his job. The reversion to his old clothes told Santo that Paolo was soliciting, probably at the *Batteria*. His reluctance to speak about his associates meant that he had something to hide.

"What kind of work are you doing?"

"The work I do best."

"And this is better than what you had at home?"

Paolo shrugged. "At home I wasn't my own boss. Here, I can someday be a boss. Let's leave it at that."

When Paolo left, Santo drank some Anisette to balance the coffee. He couldn't see how L'America had done him any good. Life wasn't simple here. With the freedom to do as one pleased, he sensed a moral loss. He saw it in the new independence of his son, in the coldness of his sister, in Pascuzzo's steady sadness, in the readiness of Vaccarella's sister-in-law to reject him because she believed he'd killed Torino and Nicolo. He saw it in the loss of his daughter, who'd moved out of Angelina's to some unknown place. What did he have here? His son, Franco, yes, but not much more. And now Paolo was gone, the man with a new name.

He went back to the storage room and lay on his cot. He stared at his pistols hung on the wall. He had no illusions about using them. His ability exceeded his will. He could hit a target at a reasonable distance, and had practiced often enough back home. But some blind pride in him refused to believe that another man would wrongfully kill him. In any case, the pistols would do little good. When men like Carmelo decided on killing it would be a surprise. The only solution was to kill him first, the ever-present solution.

He thought about what happened back home. He'd missed the killing of Nicolo by perhaps one minute. He'd been returning from the countryside, within hearing distance of the house when he heard the sound. He remembered that stark violation of the silence; the great noise of a pistol shot in the vast nothing. He'd come upon the frightened mule with its harness flying and Nicolo on the ground with part of his head missing.

But then he thought about why this death provided no satisfaction. It was the desired result by every standard. He was respected for the murder, and would have been disgraced if he'd done nothing. So why didn't he look for his daughter and then kiss her hand? She couldn't have gone far. Franco probably knew where she was, but wasn't talking. Why not reward her for redeeming herself and the family?

He didn't know how to answer these questions. Was he troubled because Mariana had taken away his valued prerogative to act? No. If he'd wanted Nicolo dead, he would have been happy with the result. The root of his troubling dissatisfaction lay not with Mariana but with himself.

Yet he couldn't make this trouble go away. He couldn't take his children back home where the March winters blew on his house, where his dear mother swaddled like a child huddled near the warm bricks of the bread oven. This was how the old ones died in Castellano. Every winter took its toll, and the children would find the American money inside a wall. Going home would be like some ridiculous reversal of action, a comedy from a movie arcade where a man cranked a filmstrip the wrong way.

He would forget Carmelo and live by his own desires. He would restore Franco's name. He would find Mariana and do the same, if she would take that name again. He would help when she most needed a father's love. Then they would present themselves to Vaccarella's sister-in-law or any other woman he liked. And if Carmelo killed him upon his return from Sicily, so be it.

CHAPTER 34

Santo heard the shatter of glass and then a great crash.

A voice in dialect cried out, "Where is that criminal?"

Santo took his pistols from the wall and crept up to the door that separated his room from the store. He saw two men. A flash came from their direction. Something stung his arm and spun him around. The men attacked him from behind. They punched and kicked him while his body registered the blows with hollow noises as he tried to breathe. Handcuffs cut into his wrists. His arm was on fire. The gas lamp was lit and he saw two policemen.

One was small and black haired. His eyes had a bloodshot look as if breathing fed a fire inside him. The second was fat. His stomach hung over his belt like a soft fruit ready to burst. He was a blond-haired, dough-faced man with an upper lip so thin it seemed no lip at all. Grasping Santo's arms, he worked him back against the bar, disregarding his cries of pain because his upper arm had been torn by a bullet.

The smaller one attacked the store as if all objects threatened his life. Using his feet and a nightstick, he swept bottles and glassware to the floor, kicked at mirrors and threw over tables and chairs. He strode into the back room and did the same. He came out sucking his knuckles.

"Where's Black Willie?"

Another blow flashed over Santo's nearly closed eye and he went down on one knee, receiving a halfhearted kick from the fat one who said, "We'll sweep you out of the city like a piece of shit."

"Enough!"

Petrosino came through the door, stepping over the litter of broken furniture as if he'd spent a lifetime walking through debris with none of it touching him. He wore the derby hat and a bright red tie. He carried a cane, which he used to remove or probe anything in his path that might soil or interest him.

He held a short cigar between two fingers and jiggled it playfully. Standing opposite Santo he said, "Now I remember. It was New Orleans where we met."

"And look at these!" said the fat one, holding up Santo's pistols.

The detective didn't ignore this, but with a slow, angry movement of his head in the officer's direction, let it be known that the remark was out of place. Then he turned to Santo, as if waiting for an explanation. Receiving none, he motioned the men outside.

Biting the cigar so all his teeth showed, Petrosino went to the store window and took down the cafe license displayed there. He folded the certificate into his pocket and said, "You have been tried and convicted for the murder of Nicolo Infante, whose mutilated body was found in a tower near the town of Castellano in the province of Palermo. The sentence imposed by the Italian court, in extenuation for a crime of passion, six years, for which the government awaits your return."

Santo wished for a speech to make these words absurd, to make this Petrosino walk out the door convinced there was another Santo Regina in New York City. But there was no way to speak. He could manage silence at best, and what might have been a look of unconcern or disbelief, he wasn't sure. His body had begun to register pain: the burning wound in his arm, the throbbing around his eyes and forehead, the cracking pain in his ribs when he took a breath, and the handcuffs, tightened directly over his wrist bone.

With all the pleasure of a victor, Petrosino seemed to be watching him think. "There is also a second offense, this more serious." He said this with a newly intensified look, as if he'd rehearsed the lines for the stage. "This murder with premeditation was committed after you left New Orleans in the company of Vito Cascio Ferro, a notorious anarchist and criminal, the force behind the notorious Black Hand. And what were you doing in New Orleans? Working for a boss named Torino, with whom you had a difference of opinion, and who was later found brutally murdered along the pier in that city, very near the spot where I saw you board the *Florida* bound for Palermo and where I observed you in the company of this Cascio Ferro. Signore Regina, you have about you the stench of crime!"

He now pulled up a chair and sitting backwards in it, continued to look Santo up and down.

"For you it's over," he said with a casual air, apparently trying different moods on Santo to see which had the most effect. "You're caught like a fish, and the question is whether I throw you back or keep you here to serve me. Six years in that stinking jail near Palermo, then back to your village in the mountains where the donkeys shit in the houses. The kind of village we all know too well."

Santo returned the detective's self-satisfied gloating with a look he hoped would convey his thoughts: that one word spoken to a man like Petrosino, even in defiance, was a compromise. Such men were convinced they knew the psychology of their opponents. Aware that his swollen lips were slurring his words, he asked a question: "Do you know why this Nicolo Infante was killed?"

Petrosino nodded sagely, as if this superior knowledge of Santo's psychology had caused him to admit the murder. "So you confess to the crime!"

"Of course I killed him! But let me ask you something: Do you have a daughter?"

Petrosino bowed his head slightly and rekindled the cigar with several short puffs. A cloud of sharp blue smoke now rose up between them.

"Do you?" he replied.

"You know the answer to that question," Santo said. "Would you like to speak with her about this 'murder' of Nicolo Infante? Or better, you should speak with her aunt, since the child would be too embarrassed to confide in a stranger. As a last offer, if you swear yourself to silence, I will tell you what I know myself. This is as far as my honor permits me to go. If you're not satisfied, send me home. Six years in a Palermo jail for an honor killing is preferable to what might happen here."

The detective shrugged and sighed with resignation. He was still appraising Santo from head to foot, as if trying to make up his mind about him. Then he took a contemplative pull on his cigar and blew the smoke downward.

"I know so many Italians from the south. This city is filled with peasants who have done something or other back home. Do you know how many ask me for favors?"

"I ask you for nothing."

Petrosino now shook his head as if he didn't need another problem. He gestured toward the front door and said, "Do you see these two men?"

"Those who destroyed my business?"

Petrosino now waved his hand violently, as if the business meant nothing compared with the point he was about to make. "These men are like certain dogs, trained to hunt one kind of animal. Sometimes they break the leash," he said, looking around the store and shaking his head with resignation. "But, they keep me honest. So I cannot throw you back in the water. You are, as a matter of fact, a stroke of luck. Your friend, Carmelo, whose brother you killed, was true to the old ways and claimed never to have seen you before."

"Do you know as much about his life as you do about mine?"

The detective put his elbows over the back of the chair and smoked the cigar pensively. "I know more," he said.

"And you are Petrosino, who believes Italians should be treated fairly. Tell me," Santo went on, knowing that speech was his only weapon now, and sensing that for some reason the detective was willing to indulge him. "What have I done in New York that your men come here like this?"

"You are an associate of Paolo Nerone, among other things."

With such men it was better not to reply to accusations, so Santo was silent. At that moment there was a noise from the street, an outburst of laughter and exuberant cries, and in the darkness Santo and the detective made out a group of boys running past the store, pushing a baby carriage and looking around furtively, brazenly disregarding the two police standing by.

Gesturing toward them as though he could determine their fate, Petrosino said, "What we do in our lives is nothing compared to what we can do for them."

"And my own children?" asked Santo. "Two who live here without a mother? You will abandon them, have them become like these thieves in the street?"

"But you see," said Petrosino, looking again toward the street, "In many ways I am helpless. The immigration knows you exist since there is now cooperation between the two countries and we receive a list of all Italian criminals who might come here. And these two police, my subordinates to be sure, they also know you exist. If I were to follow my instincts and forget I ever saw you, I could never bring them to do the same. I could bring dishonor on myself. I could lose my position at a time when this great Italian squad is beginning to do what it was designed to do. And think of the progress of our countrymen. For there is no need to tell you how the Americans think we're a race of criminals."

Petrosino shrugged as if the matter couldn't be helped. After a sidelong glance to the street he appraised Santo once more. His look was more sympathetic this time, stern, even paternal. He took out a packet of photographs, and removing a rubber band, held them up one at a time, comparing them with Santo's face. Finding no photograph which corresponded, he removed Santo's handcuffs. Putting a pencil and paper on the bar, he asked him to write something.

"Pretend this is a letter to a sweetheart. A few lines will do. Begin with *Mia Carissima*."

When this was done the detective compared the writing with that on some letters taken from his pocket. He did this quickly and with his back to Santo, holding a pair of glasses up to his eyes without fixing the ear pieces. And apparently satisfied that Santo's handwriting did not correspond to any in the letters, he said, "Very good. Now, perhaps, we can do some business."

CHAPTER 35

Mariana wore gloves with the fingers cut off below the first knuckle so she could use the scissor and needle. By the end of the day, after ten hours of snipping and hemming, her eyes were wet and tired. She napped on a pile of oddments, then walked to the flat shared with Gennaro and his sister, a blond-haired girl named Christiana.

"Tiana," who was more beautiful than her brother was handsome, had also been born in L'America. She knew English perfectly, and had been working long enough to acquire a wardrobe of clothes and shoes that Mariana envied. Tiana had arranged Mariana's job in the Grand Street shop. She also served as a legitimizing shield against her brother: the little flat had only one bed, and the women shared it. Gennaro slept in a separate room.

The shop owner, named Drushkin, reminded her of Strufolino. He was a good-natured, roly-poly fellow whose once bright red hair was beginning to absorb the grayness that came with age. Drushkin made aprons and dresses in the small shop, which comprised the front two rooms of a railroad flat. The family lived in the back room. The wife was a slender woman about two heads taller than her husband. She dressed in puffy white peasant blouses and flowered pinafores and spent her time with two young babies. On those days when she managed to make both of them nap, she came into the shop and relieved her husband on the sewing machine.

Mariana had been hired for fifty cents a day, a wage below that paid the other women. Drushkin wanted to see the speed and quality of her work before paying more. He also reminded her, through one of the other women, that her poor English was a factor in this low pay.

But Drushkin was true to his word. Mariana worked hard in the shop and practiced English with Tiana. Her salary now equaled that of the others, seventy-five cents a day. She was content. The work was tedious, but simple: to finish the dresses and aprons by sewing hems on skirts and sleeves.

Walking to the flat on King Street, taking a route along Houston or Canal, Mariana put her head into the wind and wrapped her shawl tightly around her shoulders, concentrating on those spots where her feet would step. She didn't want to look at people. It was only when she passed the butcher shop on Baxter Street that she thought of Nicolo. He said they would work in that shop. He painted a picture for her: they would be like many Italian couples in the new world, man and wife working together. And when his brother became too old to work, the business would be theirs. The thought that she once believed these promises gave her a sick feeling.

Once she went inside the shop. It reeked of guts and manure. There were droppings all over the floor and at first she recoiled from the squawks of terrified birds, a bang of cleavers, the transactions in combined English and Italian she couldn't follow. To see this wealth and work only reminded her of what a fool she'd been to believe Nicolo. Money in L'America didn't come with the snap of a finger. Would Angelo and Carmelo, who drove the butcher shop like some great engine, simply turn it over to Nicolo on demand? Work was blood. Work was death. Nicolo was a peasant who knew nothing about L'America, and now her remorse for killing him was being displaced with anger for not doing it sooner. There had never been a butcher shop for them.

She would pass by on days when her anger was strong, observing Angelo and Carmelo with gore-stained aprons over their layers of plaid and wool. She knew which was Carmelo now, the short fat man with eyes like little stones. What were his thoughts? He knew Nicolo was dead, but did he know who'd killed him? What pictures did his mind make? She couldn't imagine them. She saw only her own pictures: those where she told Carmelo that she'd killed his brother. Sometimes she was ready to do it. Her foot would take a step inside the store, but then she would correct it and continue along the street with her head hung low. She would curse herself for being afraid and make a solemn oath to someday confront the butcher.

She constructed scenes in which she entered the store and told Carmelo what had happened. She gave him details. She told him how she turned his brother into a dog. She told him how it took three days for her to work up the nerve to shoot him, three days while he passed her house with the arrogance of a baron. She would tell Carmelo about the orphanage, the nuns' insults, the child flying away on the wind.

Her iron look would wilt him. He would be unable to speak and she would walk out of the store leaving him dumbfounded.

Soon his friends and enemies, hearing of this visit, would tell him exactly what they knew of the story. Perhaps that woman, Andrea, the worldly-wise prostitute from Palermo, would write him a letter. Carmelo would then come to the boarding house with hat in hand. He would forgive her for killing his brother.

When she thought about Nicolo her limbs weakened with shame. She wanted to eliminate herself from the world, reach into her stomach and rip out her insides, discard herself, evaporate into the biting city wind. He'd dominated her with one idea: L'America. *Take her inside you!* What an unspeakable fool she'd been for that beautiful Italian word! That little piece of music on everyone's lips had opened the way to a degradation not only unspeakable but also unoriginal. This was the most painful part, the delusion that their common lovemaking in the clearing with the brook flowing by was something never seen before, something only they could know.

Then she met Gennaro, whose past was more sin-ridden and degraded than her own. He'd been to a reform school after being repeatedly caught for stealing. He told her what it was like among boys, what parts of others had entered into him, what parts of him had entered others. He whispered to her of the textures and lubrications of sin. He had the zeal of an obsessed priest speaking of miracles. Mariana said nothing about herself, choosing to gather both their sins around her like a garland of flowers.

"You've been with a man before," he said.

"Never."

"I don't believe you, but I don't care either. I don't care what you've done."

He looked at her, then away. He'd sworn to respect her until they married. This was why he insisted they sleep in different parts of the flat. During the time they'd been together they hadn't gone beyond kissing.

Gennaro worked in construction and brought home fifteen dollars a week. He presented this to Mariana and she planned the budget, always putting a little aside to repay Angelina when the time was right. Gennaro went to Mass every Sunday and even confided his living situation to a priest, who promised to arrange the marriage. And he liked nothing better than to walk with Mariana along the Hudson River, holding her hand while they gazed at the freighters and ocean liners moored there.

One day they were at the *Batteria* when a ferry arrived from Ellis Island. It was a cold, bitter day, and the peddlers selling hot chestnuts, gloves, and scarves were doing a good business. Mariana and Gennaro joined the crowd. Many held up signs with the names of the new arrivals they were supposed to meet. Then the immigrants came out. Some had chalk marks on their clothing. Others had tags tucked into their hatbands or hanging from their buttons. Many of the youngsters were shaven nearly bald as part of a delousing process recently adopted by the Italian government.

This was a time for emotion: fear, love, confidence, meekness, brashness. One man in a full-length fur coat came out in the open and sang a song to the crowd in a language said to be Russian. He was soon accompanied by two Italians with guitar and mandolin, the trio having had the voyage to practice. Gulls overhead cried into the wind blowing up from the harbor. The immigrants kept pouring out of the Barge Office, crowding the reception area in front.

A little boy in a suit wrinkled and soiled from the journey ran from his parents to a place beyond the edge of the crowd. He began kicking at the stones and dirt.

"He's looking for money!" said his mother, her voice both stern and tragic, as if their son had once again displayed his weak mind. She looked skyward and clasped her hands, as if only God could help. Her husband, who'd taken off after the boy, cuffed him on the back of the head and picked him up by the jacket collar, presenting him to the group of relatives he'd insulted by naively looking for money on the ground. These relatives, experienced Americans already, laughingly admitted that upon their own arrival they too had looked for coins in the street.

Mariana watched these scenes intently, no longer aware that she was arm-in-arm with Gennaro. She overheard someone say that two and three steamships were unloading every day. She looked at these new people, especially the women, as a combat veteran might watch the coming of replacements. They would get what they asked for. There would be work for those backs and fingers.

As part of the exuberance of the moment, the crowd began clapping for the new arrivals. The musicians struck up a tarantella. People cried "*Viva L'America!*" Others called out in opposition, "*Mannaggia L'America!*" Mariana sang out the latter cry as well. Curse America! Damn America!

Why did she want to curse America? Because it wasn't like home. But that didn't matter now. So many had joined the chorus. The musicians were soon joined by a violinist, who also sang folk songs and operatic arias. It was only when gusts of wind blew papers and dust clouds that the crowd broke up.

Mariana and Gennaro continued their walk, hands in each other's pockets.

"Marry me now," he said. "I told my father about you."

"Does he think I'm a *puttana* for living with you?"

"My sister has given you a good report. Most important of all, my father has seen the change since being with you. I'm no longer a thief."

Mariana said nothing for a long time. The wind at their backs swept down her neck, but despite this painful cold she detached herself from Gennaro's warmth and walked alone, head tucked into her shoulders. Wisps of her long black hair blew out in front of her.

Gennaro had proposed several times. She always refused to answer. She liked him less since he'd changed. What would be the difference between marriage to him and life with Angelina? He was gentle now. But later he would chain her like a dog. This much about men she knew already. She thought of Olga, the flower maker from Posillipo; of Tiana, who swore never to marry, but to use men for whatever they had to offer. How did these women avoid having babies? This was a trick Angelina had not explained well enough.

Gennaro moved back and took her hand. He tried to put the hand around his waist and into his coat pocket again.

"No, don't."

"What's the matter?"

"Nothing."

"I don't understand why you cursed back there. Why did you curse America? Did something happen to you here?"

"It was a game. Everyone was doing it."

"But the others were joking. You were serious. Are you so unhappy here?"

She shrugged. To say she was unhappy here would be to admit weakness. Men like Gennaro would eventually exploit weakness. But to say she was happy would be a lie. What was more, Gennaro might consider himself the cause of this and press her even harder for marriage. Why had she cursed America? Maybe because she resented those poor foreigners because they had the option of going back.

A gust of wind pushed her from behind. She at least had been lucky enough to arrive in America during warm weather. The idea of starting a new life in this cold, of being homeless on the freezing streets, as many would be, tempered her frustration. She felt lucky now to have a job and a place to live.

"I'm not so unhappy," she said.

Gennaro took her hand and thrust it into his pocket. She didn't resist this time, and in a reciprocal gesture, locked her fingers with his. He was exciting again. He was learning about her. In some vague way she could picture their lives together, a combination of regularity and unpredictability. She wanted him to take her back to the flat then. Tiana was gone. There was enough coal to warm the rooms. She could take a chance with the blood. But then he said something that turned her cold.

"I'd like to meet your father."

Behind the innocence of his tone there was not only a command, but an assumption they would need her father's blessing for marriage.

"He's not my father," she said.

Gennaro looked at her as if she didn't realize what an outrage she'd spoken. She returned the look. Could someone who'd once ruled a gang of Italian boys be such a *mammalucco*? Could someone born here behave like a peasant from the mountains?

"He's not my father," she repeated.

"Why?"

"Because he says the same about me: that I'm not his daughter."

"Who tells you this?"

"My brother, my aunt, everyone. They say that if he sees me in the street, he'll kill me."

"No man can kill his daughter."

"Then he will beat me and give me scars. You don't know what he's done."

"Apologize to him," Gennaro said.

"For what?"

"This is a question you must answer."

Her hand closed on itself in his pocket, then came out. She put her head down and walked. She had to be on her own, away from Gennaro, away from her father. This would mean working harder for Drushkin. She would show him what an Italian could do. After that, she would repay Angelina, get a room of her own, and tell Carmelo who'd killed his brother. Then there would be no debts.

The man she wanted would ask no questions, make no demands. He would love her without anger, but not too softly either, not so softly as Gennaro.

CHAPTER 36

Santo entered the lobby and squinted at the light from numerous gas lamps. As he climbed a circular flight of marble steps he was struck by the gold-like fabric which covered the walls and reflected the light. The detective lived well. Once on the first landing Santo stopped before the next staircase. The steps were straight and steep. He extended his good arm along the bannister as if aiming himself upward, then rested his head on the arm and listened to the hissing of the gas lamps.

After a few moments he found the energy to mount the steps. He stopped at every landing to catch his breath. His body was trying to repair itself. He was also angry, and anger had a way of taking his strength: Mariana's disappearance now appeared to be permanent.

He'd come to this expensive building to meet with Petrosino, who hadn't arrested him on the night his store was wrecked, but had invited him to dinner instead. It seemed the detective liked him. Now Santo wished he could take his old fashioned morality by the neck and throw it in the river. A smarter man would be halfway to California by now. To hell with his children! To hell with trust! His son could survive as Franco Savino. And as for the daughter-who-no-longer-existed, survival was her own business. He would never see her again.

But he was here. He would clear the name. He would end the uncertainty. It would come down to a bargain, and when he reached Petrosino's apartment door he was struck by the smell of Italian cooking. It was that familiar combination of sweetness and pungency, most likely peppers fried in olive oil. The aroma of cooking entered the deepest parts of his being. Yet it seemed strange to smell this food in a place where Italians weren't to be found, for this was a building at some remove from the tenement area. This aroma so reminiscent of home, family, love, and security, now instilled a sense of loss. His business was ruined. His daughter had run away. His simple desire to make a proper home had become complicated and unattainable.

The door was opened by a tall woman with mixed gray hair swept back into a bun. She wore a cameo necklace. Set into the stone was a tiny photograph of a man's face—probably a dead man, for this was the custom with that kind of jewelry. She greeted him wordlessly, and after taking his coat and hat, indicated the living room where the back of Petrosino's partly bald head stuck up from a sofa upon which a holstered pistol hung over the back. The detective sat before a fire of glowing red coals. A shotgun hung above the mantel with a pair of duck decoys below.

Petrosino greeted Santo warmly and with some informality, inquiring about his wound as if it were no more significant than the time of day. Then he indicated a table in the dining room, where the tall woman was already setting down dishes of food.

The detective seemed completely interested in the meal, which he ate in great deference to the woman who'd let Santo in. The cooking was too oily for Santo's taste, but he ate with a show of appreciation. The detective asked him if he liked every dish, and seemed to be testing him, as if absolute love of this woman's food might be the price of his freedom.

During the meal Petrosino told stories about his police work, but these were never rendered to completion. Either the arrival of something else to eat, or a similarity between one story and the next, would cause him to jump from one adventure to another. Petrosino looked at Santo intently when he switched narratives, as if testing the younger man's memory.

According to him, Italian criminals had created the expressions Black Hand, mafia, and camorra. These were terms of convenience, with no palpable function except to frighten victims.

"You won't believe how ruthless these men have been," he said, enumerating how he had personally solved many crimes committed by individuals and gang members. Some of these successes took place before the famous Italian Squad existed, when Petrosino worked alone, often ridiculed as the "Italian Expert."

Petrosino showed him a scrapbook of photographs and newspaper clippings. This was a record of his police career, from patrolman to detective. Banner headlines and photo collages told of his victories: how, for example, he'd deported Enrico "Big Henry" Alfano, a leader in the Neapolitan camorra. Petrosino had arranged for reporters to be on hand when he made the arrest, alone.

Elaborating on each story, stressing how the newspapers were inaccurate and never willing to give him his due, Petrosino described his capture of the Insurance Gang, a group that sold life insurance to fellow Italians, with one stipulation: in exchange for their low rates, one of the gang was always named as beneficiary. When this was done they would murder the insured and collect the money. There were numerous individuals arrested and deported—thieves, extortionists, murderers—men whose victims were almost always Italians. Petrosino stressed that he solved these crimes because he was a student of southern Italian psychology.

The detective wasn't modest about his achievements. He'd been promoted from patrolman to detective by Theodore Roosevelt, now President, but then Police Commissioner.

"How many Italians do you know who can use the telephone to speak with the President of the United States?" he asked.

This subject led him to discuss anarchism among Italian immigrants. Most of the anarchists were in Paterson, New Jersey, a community the detective claimed to have penetrated by disguising himself as a peddler. He told Santo how he'd warned both Presidents McKinley and Roosevelt of anarchist plots to assassinate them.

"But McKinley didn't listen. Why? Because he underestimated my ability!"

He set the scrapbook aside and looked up at Santo like a man of great importance who'd invited to dinner a man of no importance. Santo looked at him, then past him, through a window to the building across the street. It was a new building with new bricks and wrought iron balconies. This was a rich country and Petrosino had made himself part of it. Santo, on the other hand, was part of neither country. His fate depended on this man, who would exact a price for his freedom. He looked at the detective and said, "Tell me what you want."

Petrosino placed his hand on Santo's knee. It was a paternal gesture. The detective would control and protect him. He gripped the knee tightly and said, "You will serve me."

Santo looked from the detective's imploring face to the hand which had relaxed its grip. That hand now patted his knee affectionately as if the answer was already given as yes.

"Why do you want me to serve you?"

"To give you a chance to redeem yourself. Besides, you're the only man for the job I need to do. You also have reason to do it."

"The reason?"

"Your murder of Nicolo Infante."

"And the job?"

"It would be impossible to tell you everything now, but I will say as much as I can. If we are successful, if you play your part, all scores will be settled, between you, me, and our mutual friend, the butcher from Baxter Street. You will be able to remain in L'America, living with no fear for yourself or your family."

The detective held out his palms as if no human being could offer more.

"Let me express myself in another way," he said. "Any number of men are willing and perhaps able to do the job I ask of you. But if I were to dream of the ideal man, it would be you. And here is why: among the quarter million Italians being dumped into this city by their government every year, there are too many for a man like myself to help. All these men have the Italian mentality: they live life with two schemes. The first lies on the surface: it is the man's public plan for living, that he will work a certain job, live in a certain place, behave in a certain way. But there is a second scheme, the private one, a man's insurance against the blows of life. These are the little thieveries, the uses of influence, the lies, the measure of dishonesty by which he greases the wheels. It isn't so difficult to discover this part of any man.

"I believe you are a man without this second scheme. You go through life believing other men will pay homage to your quality, and that you don't need to lower yourself to immorality. This is why you went to the butcher shop: you thought to intimidate Carmelo with the force of truth. And in fact you did! Our friend is in Sicily at this very moment, trying to discover what we already know, and what he refuses to believe: that his brother wasn't killed by you, but by your daughter."

"And how do you know this?" Santo asked.

"From your sister, an intelligent woman who knows how to make friends with the police. Come now, there's no need to lie anymore. Your lie has served its purpose, to get your children out of Sicily.

And why you didn't go to Carmelo with the truth is something I can understand, but something impossible to do right now."

"Where is he?"

Petrosino put one finger to his temple and made a circular motion to indicate Carmelo's disillusion.

"In Sicily, learning 'the truth.' And there he will remain until I approve the papers for his return."

Santo stood up and went to the window. This part of the city was as different from the Italian section as night and day. There were trees and grassy places on the sidewalks. He saw flowers, shrubbery, carriages with paired horses waiting to provide service to women with their hands in furry muffs, or to men with ties and canes.

He heard the detective say, "Don't worry. I will talk to Carmelo. Everything will be settled."

Santo turned to him. "This is what you are telling me, and although I have committed no crime, you will do nothing to support my innocence, and in fact will do everything to falsely deport me, unless I serve you in some way that you have yet to specify."

"Exactly," replied the detective, inspecting a small red and yellow apple. He passed it under his nose, then held it up to communicate its quality.

Santo said, "At the same time, you would reveal the truth to Carmelo, with the hope he will allow me and my family to live in peace."

"Not the hope," said Petrosino, making two cuts into the apple and pulling out a neat quarter. "This will be a condition of Carmelo's return. The butcher wasn't aware when he went to Sicily that I had the power to prevent his return."

"I want to refuse you," Santo said, "Not because you're going to endanger my life, or even because you'll ask me to do something against my nature. But most of all I want to refuse because you've played with me. And let me tell you, six years in a Sicilian prison wouldn't be hard to do. And with the help of my family and friends the sentence may be greatly reduced, given the state of the law in our ridiculous country. But before I refuse, I need to know your plan. What exactly do you want of me?"

The apple quarter now skinned and seeded, Petrosino held it up and said, "The man I hope to trap is your friend from New Orleans."

"What friend?"

"Vito Cascio Ferro, of course. He'll remember a man who saved his life. And had you known what murder and violence he incited in L'America, had you known the innocent Italians whose stores were bombed, whose means of livelihood were destroyed, or those shot and butchered in the most brutal fashion, you would have gone the other way when you met this man in New Orleans. He was in L'America for one year, one small year! And in that time he was able to examine the kind of society we have, and persuade these bandits to operate in a way nearly impossible to counteract. No longer do these Black Hand extortionists send a letter to a businessman demanding five hundred dollars and threatening to bomb his store or kill his children. Now everything is nice-nice, everything is *bus-i-ness*! Five dollars every week, two dollars every week, all quiet, all friends, no trouble. Five dollars for what? To belong to our club. Give the club a holy name. Give the club the name of a town. Have one feast every year. Everybody happy, even the police. And whose idea was all this? That of 'Don' Vito Cascio Ferro.

"I nearly had my hands on him in New Orleans but for you! And this is another reason why you should serve me. These stupid American laws! Invented by aristocrats who assumed new immigrants would be like themselves!" exclaimed the detective, now raising his voice and pointing downward with his index finger to emphasize his words. "Vito Cascio Ferro is afraid! This is why he hasn't shown his face in this country since then! And this is why I will go to Sicily and bring him back myself!"

"So you would put me in a trap."

The detective abruptly sat forward, holding out his hands and gesturing in order to make his case.

"What man isn't trapped? Who do you think traps me? On one side is the police inspector, an Irish who drives me like a beast, who is ready to stop all Italians from coming to this country. Listen my friend, do you think I have a personal vendetta? The fate of thousands of poor Italians who want a better life rests upon my ability to prove that Italians are human beings who know how to keep their bodies as clean as anyone else, and perhaps cleaner. Because at this point in history, we are considered as low as the blacks.

"And who else traps me besides my Irish boss? These shits I am trying to flush out of the country before they stab me forty times and stuff me into a barrel, as your friend the noble Don did to that poor man a few years back. And while he didn't commit the crime personally, he ordered it as directly as a man buys a tomato."

The detective sat back and looked at Santo as if satisfied that he'd won the argument.

"I am a man who knows Presidents," he cautioned, "not some Neapolitan braggart. And before I explain this plan, I will demonstrate my power to you."

He produced a large brown envelope, withdrew a sheaf of papers, and passed them over. Santo couldn't read English, but he recognized his name, along with official seals and titles from the New York Police, the Bureau of Immigration, and the Italian Ministry of Justice.

"These are your deportation papers. What remains is for me to testify that you are unfit to lawfully live in American society. And this would be easy to do, considering your association with men who engage in prostitution. Your friend Paolo Nerone for one. And if I were to relate the scheme used to enslave innocent girls, you in particular would want to cut off his hands."

Santo couldn't move. He felt a discord within as fear curbed his anger, one wave overcoming another and making him powerless. Petrosino had learned to work in L'America. How often had the detective watched the jaws of a trap close around his man? Paolo was surely in jail already, and Santo was sorry for this, for he didn't believe his friend was as heartless as Petrosino made him out.

Changing his tone of voice to a more fatherly one, Petrosino said, "You have every right to doubt me. But the wheels are in motion. You can send a message to your family. They can bring a lawyer to look at these papers. But whatever your decision, it's merely a question of where you sleep tonight: at the Ellis Island jail, or in this apartment, a more pleasant jail. Two men will be here to treat you well. In either case, you are under arrest. A steamship leaves tomorrow for Genoa, Naples, and Palermo. You will be on it. You will be given specific instructions. Follow them and you can return here. Ignore them and you will be a Sicilian for the rest of your life."

CHAPTER 37

Santo awoke when the engines stopped and the steamship slid into the dock at Palermo. He kept to one side of his bunk to avoid the network of asbestos-wrapped piping hung from the ceiling and dripping rust-colored water. Below him in less troubled repose lay Paolo Nerone, deported for good. Perhaps this was why he slept so well.

Santo sat on an empty bunk nearby, rubbing the beard he hadn't shaved in three weeks as a way to mark time and perhaps bring him luck. It hadn't worked. He was tormented every night by a dream in which Petrosino and Don Vito held his arms and pulled him in opposite directions. He looked around him. The steerage compartment was only half full. Mattresses on the empty bunks were rolled up. Most of the passengers were rejects, turned back at Ellis Island for old age, lack of money, or suspicion of disease. Others had made their money and were going home. There were also several younger men—Paolo among them—who'd either been deported or turned back because they were undesirable in some other way.

The compartment reeked of coal gas and unwashed humanity. People hadn't bathed for weeks. Yet modesty more than lack of facilities prevented them from using the bank of washing sinks along one wall into which trickled some rusty water. The only relief from the human odor came when someone revolted to the limit threw open the cabin doors on both sides, flushing the compartment with the freezing sea breeze. When this became intolerable the doors were shut, allowing the smells to accumulate once more.

Paolo had a cold and slept with his mouth open, his breath whistling through the new space in his front teeth. Two of them were missing, the result of a beating by Petrosino and his men on the day after Santo and the detective had dinner. Either from spite or ignorance, Paolo hadn't revealed the names and whereabouts of the men who'd contrived the prostitution scheme in which he'd played a part.

After Paolo awoke, the two men stood at the outside rail and looked at their old city. A thick fog wrapped itself around the nearly sheer face of Monte Pellegrino and pressed down on the city. At the base of the mountain, in the flat port area, the fog pushed into the ranks of the assorted craft moored there—fishing skiffs with eyes painted on their prows, larger, two-masted boats with netted rigging, and a pair of single-stack steamships. With the arrival of a boat from America, a crowd began to gather on the pier.

More passengers appeared along the rail, preferring the breezy, cold air to the malignant smell of the cabin. Some came to air out clothing, which they either hung from pre-strung ropes or simply held up to the breeze. Some began waving to people gathering on the pier. There were others, undisturbed by the mounting excitement, who came out to continue their sleep, arranging their bedding on warm bulkheads, or near any surface that radiated heat.

Through the swirling fog Santo saw the general form of the city, a bedrock of low buildings like ranks of children's blocks, a once-simple geometry now a base for domes, towers, and *palazzi* rising like tiered wedding cakes. A necklace of flat plains taken up by citrus groves surrounded the city. Beyond lay the Madonie Mountains, Castellano, his mother, the step-by-step way of life. Carmelo was poking around somewhere in all that landscape. Or perhaps he was in Palermo. Santo told himself to be careful. He could be the victim in this master plan. Petrosino didn't care if he lived or died. He was obsessed with the "thousands" of Italian criminals he imagined would infect L'America if Don Vito went free.

The docking steamship drew assorted vendors and peddlers to the pier. They arrived in carts pulled by donkeys, ponies, even goats. Others came on foot and balanced sacks and baskets on their heads. They were selling fresh water, fruits, nuts, various sweets, all arranged attractively and with a level of primping and fussing far beyond the value of the goods themselves. Observing this energetic group of men hoping for a sale of any kind, Santo became aware of the scaled-down life in Sicily. The peddlers took up their cries with that familiar anger and unflagging desperation: the goods, the prices. It would be some time before the passengers were allowed to disembark, but still these men hawked their bargains. One peddler pushed a stove mounted on wheels to the edge of the pier. The stove already glowed with a charcoal fire. With exaggerated movements and a kind of chanting, the peddler sprinkled some oil into a brass pot. He applied spices with a flourish, working his hands over the pot as if these herbs had materialized from thin air. He began throwing large red and green peppers into the pot, holding up each one to display their quality. The sweet, distinctive aroma of this oily roasting soon came up on the wind, causing Paolo to make his first remark of the day: "I'm in the wrong business."

Santo shivered with cold and hunger. A gust cleared part of Monte Pellegrino's steep face then swept out over the water. More fog swirled around the mountain to fill the void. Was he any more than a hungry mouth on this planet, some shivering ant on a feeble twig crossing a body of God's water? He'd nurtured his hurts as if they were sacred and exceptional. Yet he never admitted that he was inadequate to God's great gift, never admitted his inadequacy as a father. He'd lost his daughter. He was nearly a stranger to a son growing into manhood. Without a father, and luckily with the guidance of Angelina and Pascuzzo, his son was learning the value of hard work. Franco could swim the streets of New York like a fish.

Both his children had assumed Santo would bear the burden of Nicolo's death. Why not? He'd asked for that burden with his silence. He'd posed as a killer and this was an easy part to play. But there was a price. Men like Don Vito and Petrosino singled him out because they saw him as one of them, a man of respect and justice, but also a man capable of murder.

Santo turned to Paolo, who rested his elbows on the rail and set his chin in his hands.

"What are you thinking?"

"About what will happen to us."

Santo wanted to console Paolo without saying anything false. "The detective might change his mind about you. I can speak with him."

"No!" Paolo turned abruptly, touching the space where his largest front teeth had been. On Paolo this gap looked especially grotesque because his mouth now closed completely, and his lips didn't seem to know what to do. Several times during the voyage he complained bitterly of Petrosino's brutality. Santo had seen a change taking place from the accommodating man he once knew. Paolo was now angry.

"You know yourself," said Paolo, "that even with the face of a toothless old man I can return to L'America whenever I want since immigration law is still in confusion. He cannot keep me out and will get what he deserves. And for this I must warn you. Be careful what you do and how far you risk yourself for someone who merely uses you. Petrosino's mission is not so secret as he thinks. And mark me, what he's trying to do will offend many proud men."

Touching the space between his teeth once again for emphasis, Paolo said, "Do you know why this was done? Not because my crime was so despicable. Not because these 'innocent' girls were brought here for prostitution. This was done because his great Italian Squad was a failure. He has deported only twenty men so far. Three just escaped from the jail at Ellis Island. And this from a list of three thousand names."

"How do you know this?"

"Because each time he hit me he said, 'Three thousand men! And you are just the beginning!' This has been in the newspapers. Petrosino's reputation will rise and fall on the number of Italians he deports, guilty or innocent. For example, what proof do you have that he will allow you back into the country? Nothing but his word. Do you trust it?"

"I have no choice. I want to be near my children."

"There! Only his word!" And with an angry motion of his hand, Paolo indicated that his point had been made.

They shook hands on the pier, and just as he'd done when they met in L'America, Santo watched a less optimistic Paolo walk away. On that day in L'America Paolo had been looking at his surroundings. Here he walked with his head down, occasionally waving off the peddlers who accosted him.

CHAPTER 38

Santo followed the waterfront toward the Piazza Marina and the hotel *Venezia* where Petrosino had instructed him to stay. During the short walk to the hotel he was solicited by several men who assumed he'd gotten rich in L'America. Santo rejected them politely and with such confidence that they soon gave up.

Aware of someone else suddenly walking close behind, he stopped and turned. He faced a younger man with a bowler hat and a pleasant, boyish smile. Placing his thumbs in both vest pockets, the man said, "Have you come from the steamship?"

"No," said Santo, thinking him another solicitor. He turned and continued toward the hotel. But the young man followed even more closely. As Santo turned to speak to him once more, he was aware of a horse-drawn cab keeping their pace. The driver labored to restrain his horse and when the cab stopped a figure beckoned him from inside.

"Don't worry," said the young man to Santo. "This is a friend of yours."

The cab door opened and Don Vito came forward into the light. He looked younger than Santo's memory of him from New Orleans. His short gray hair was just long enough to sustain a part in the middle. His mustaches, more in accord with Sicilian custom, were longer. From the open door he held out two arms and guided Santo into the opposite seat. After dismissing the young man, he tapped the roof of the cab with his cane and they started forward. Once they were under way he studied Santo with the calm satisfaction of a man in his element, then reached over and patted him on the knee.

"I know what that *schifoso* detective is holding over you."

Santo was about to say that he didn't know what would happen, when Don Vito raised his hand, indicating that apologies or explanations were unnecessary.

"Let me take you along the port," he said. "It's a pleasant drive. The sun is coming up, and later we can return to your hotel."

As they passed the docks crowded with fishing boats, the cab stopped several times while the don greeted peddlers, fishermen, and shopkeepers. Many presented the don with gifts—bread, cakes, top quality fruit. Before long a straw basket on the seat was filled. Santo noted that the conversations with these men were pleasant and cordial. They spoke of the weather, of business, of their families. There was nothing sinister in the don's tone of voice. Santo wondered whether this display of patronage was for his benefit.

They drove around the port for some time. There was no mention of Petrosino. When the cab stopped in front of the *Venezia*, Santo looked up. Don Vito returned his look, as if Santo should provide the explanation.

"How much do you know?" asked Santo.

"About you, enough. I know why you went to L'America, and why your life is in danger from more quarters than you think. Your friend Carmeluzzo sniffs around the mountains like a dog obsessed with a single rabbit. Meanwhile the famous detective holds a pistol at your head. And those he deported are waiting for him with blood in their eyes." The don sighed as if some unpleasant chore was coming.

"Does Carmelo know who killed his brother?" asked Santo.

"Perhaps. There's a rumor he'll stay up there," the don said, gesturing toward the mountains. "He has a few enemies, but they're old, like him. Now that he's lost a brother they may leave him alone. Who can tell about men?"

"What would you do in my place?"

Don Vito's slate-colored eyes looked steadily at Santo. They seemed to penetrate him as deeply as they opened a way into Don Vito himself. So stark was their expression that Santo could barely maintain eye contact. But then the don looked away. He worked his mouth as if tasting something he didn't like, and in these gestures Santo smelled the odor of corruption and even deception. Don Vito looked back at Santo sharply, perhaps realizing that the younger man had sensed something, had seen through his spell. His source of power had always been some inexplicable hypnotic effect, something that had won Santo over in Castellano and in New Orleans. Santo watched him stroke his long mustaches and flatten them against his chin.

Don Vito pushed the cab door open with his foot, but when Santo moved to exit, Don Vito pulled the door shut. He was angry, his face red. Santo recalled how livid he'd turned when he discovered

Petrosino had been asking for him in the streets of New Orleans, making his name public.

"What do you want?" asked Santo. "What will happen here?"

The Don spoke with a didactic, impatient quality, as if Santo were slow to realize the magnitude of Petrosino's offense. His voice almost a whisper, he told Santo that Petrosino—and he didn't use his name—was one in a long line of police presuming to impose the will of Rome on Sicilians. None of these men had left the country alive. He cited several by name, counting them off on his fingers, as if reciting the law of the land. The last mentioned was the *carabiniere* Finelli, killed while chasing Carmelo.

When the Don spoke this name he arched one eyebrow to drive the lesson home.

"Do you know about the infamous Finelli?"

"'Who doesn't?"

"Your detective speaks too freely to the newspapers. He'll soon be here to prevent passage to L'America for those who turned to petty crime for reasons of the stomach. These he would deprive of a better life. He would keep them here against the force of history."

Santo looked directly into the Don's face contorted in anger. He felt fortunate that Petrosino's only instructions were for him to check into the *Venezia*. There he would wait for Petrosino on the next steamship. Santo would be unable to lie if Don Vito asked for details. He listened as more whispered words washed over him in the confinement and half-light of the cab. Don Vito was pronouncing on sin, pride, and above all, vanity. Santo didn't know what role he was playing in this game between the two men, and for a moment he closed his eyes and imagined his transfer to death.

But if he lived, what would he say of these moments in the dark carriage at the port of Palermo, where his view of the sea through the cab window might be his last? When Mariana and Franco asked how he'd survived, would he be silent? Would he gesture wordlessly, like the man of respect, whose secret of life could never be imparted, but which must grow in his children from within? Or would he remove his mask and tell them how his fear of death was so strong that he lost all feeling in his limbs?

Don Vito might have been praying. There were no ups and downs in his tone of voice, only the logic of his words, uttered like the benediction of a priest weary of sin.

"And why would this detective take food from the families of poor Sicilians? I'll tell you. Not only because he is ambitious to be the Commissioner of Police in the English city of New York. But because he is a victim of his own propaganda. He believes the southern Italian is prone to crime."

The don shrugged and looked upward as if the folly of man would never cease. He opened the door. Santo stepped down and took his extended hand.

"You once did a favor for a man in New Orleans," said the don. His manner was stern, and since he said no more, Santo grasped his meaning: friendship between them was no longer possible because the favor had been repaid in ways Santo would soon discover.

Don Vito pulled shut the carriage door and as a parting gesture put one finger under his right eye. "Be careful," he said.

Then he signaled the driver to move along.

CHAPTER 39

Santo found the gate to his house open but the door locked. The potted plants on the balcony had died long ago and now bent stiffly in the March wind. He unlocked the basement hatch and crawled inside over hay bundles cut a year ago. The room had a clean, unused smell, the sweet hay preventing it from becoming musty or sour. There was no dust. Harness, jars, bottles, the big wine barrel, all intact. He tapped the barrel with a wooden spigot and filled a jar, sitting up on the cart while he took a sip. The wine hadn't turned and he drank some more, feeling warm, then slightly dizzy. He looked around. His hand tools still hung on the wall, the tools were old friends now, no longer associated with toil, but with nostalgia for the simple life. He hefted a small sickle, caressing the smooth handle, touching the greased blade. Franco had left everything in order.

The rooms were clean and empty. His mother sometimes went to stay with some cousins in the town, especially when bad weather was coming. An empty pitcher and basin had been set in the shutter-darkened window where Mariana and his mother had huddled after Nicolo's death. There were new photographs on the walls, those of the Americans: Angelina and Pascuzzo, Franco and Mariana together on the roof at Elizabeth Street, himself outside the store on the west side. He wore a white apron that came down to his shoes, and he was squinting into the sun.

He climbed up to his room and went through the pressboard trunk, feeling the familiar embroidered sheets, handmade lace, baby clothes, a wedding dress. He carried the trunk downstairs. It would go back to L'America.

He started up to town on foot, holding his hat so it wouldn't blow off. His mother would be there, perhaps with cousins. This was the time of year when people stayed inside and counted their sticks of wood and stores of food. The chill wind pushed long gray clouds across the sky. More clouds moving up from the valleys flung down a mix of snow and rain.

Santo didn't see the animal until he was even with it, and then only the legs caught his eye. They belonged to a gray mule with red speckles, an animal soaked from the weather and with muddy streaks down its legs. It was tall, as good mules can be taller than horses. This one had short ears and alert eyes. Its rider had stopped to urinate against the retaining wall on the roadside. He was a short, burly man with leather boots laced to the knees. His dark clothes blended into the rocks and brush. The man now turned around, still buttoning his trousers. It was Carmelo in his butcher-store hat—here in the mountains of Sicily—the dark blue fedora with the brim turned up all around.

Santo drew his pistol and aimed for Carmelo's heart. He was too far away for an accurate shot but he didn't want to take his eyes from Carmelo, not even for an instant. He stood fast as the rain and snow continued. Thunder cracked so sharply that he and Carmelo both jumped, but the mule—showing great poise—simply looked toward the source of the noise with pricked ears.

Carmelo finished buttoning up as if Santo didn't exist. Then he gestured at the pistol and said, "What the hell are you doing with that?"

Santo lowered the pistol, but then raised it higher. His hand shook. He told himself that he was here, on this side of the ocean, in this unpopulated countryside, facing someone who'd been hunting him. Yet he couldn't shoot, not because he might miss at the distance, but because Nicolo had deserved his death and Carmelo should recognize that.

Carmelo held up two empty hands and said, "Why did you come back here?"

"To see whether you've learned the truth."

Carmelo waved as if to disregard this unnecessary concern. Then he grasped the reins under the mule's chin and led it toward the retaining wall, where he could step in order to mount. But he didn't mount. The big animal stood sideways to Santo now, with Carmelo behind it. A two-barreled *lupara* came down over the saddle. The hammers clicked one at a time.

"I knew the truth in L'America," he said. "Your daughter told me the truth."

Santo spoke into the black holes of the weapon. "Why do you believe her?"

"She came into my store on Baxter Street and told me everything.

Of course, I didn't believe her at first. I thought she was trying to protect you."

"And do you believe her now?"

"I've spoken to many people, including a woman friend named Giuseppina—a friend of your daughter from the laundry pool. I've spoken to Paolo Nerone and the nuns at the orphanage in Palermo."

"And do you want to kill me now?"

Carmelo shrugged. "I ask you the same about me."

Santo kept his pistol up. "What do you believe?"

"I know there was a child, and I knew my little brother. He was weak, and a pig. Put away your pistol, Regina. The most you can do is put a hole in this fine animal, for which I've paid a great deal of money."

Rain dripped from Santo's hat brim as he watched Carmelo for any abrupt movement. He imagined being tricked after he put down his pistol. The world would explode in his face. This was how such men worked. Carmelo had shrugged his shoulders as if to say that nothing could be done. Santo shuddered from the cold. His fingers were stiff from holding the pistol. Death came to the weary, to the straggler in the herd, to the man tired of fighting who lowers his guard. Here was an addition to the legend: Carmelo tells him to drop his pistol, then shoots him dead. He joins Finelli, dead with the righteous. He glanced upward, at the sheer, mortared stone and nearly windowless wall of Castellano's perimeter.

"Do you believe my daughter killed your brother?"

"Yes, of course."

"And what do you say? What do you think of this?"

"My brother lived and died. Knowing your daughter as I do, he deserved his death. Had I been here, the issue would have been forced. They would have been married, with your consent of course. Satisfied now? Put up the pistol, I'm too old for trouble." He broke open the *lupara* and put the shells in his pocket.

Santo lowered the pistol. He watched as the weapon slid out of sight. Then Carmelo signaled that he wanted to speak.

"Many told me about your daughter, even your mother, who now lies in the cemetery. I'm sorry if you didn't know this, but she died a few weeks ago. You would have been crossing over from the other side.

Before her death she called me to her house and swore by everything holy that you didn't do it. How do the old ones die? They fall asleep on a cold night. The fire goes out and they never wake up."

The pistol resting against Santo's leg began to shake. He felt the pressure of tears behind his eyes and turned sideways to hide them.

"I'm sorry about that," said Carmelo, gathering the reins. The mule came to attention, and with surprising agility, Carmelo vaulted into the saddle by stepping first on the wall. "I won't see you in New York. I make my life here." He started downhill, then stopped and pointed to Santo's pistol.

"You may need that in Palermo."

"The detective!" cried Santo. "What do you know?"

Carmelo pulled up and shook his head as if to throw off a bad memory. He moved one hand in a slow, circular motion, the sign of death. Then he said, "It has already happened!" and trotted away.

CHAPTER 40

Franco headed home in the bread cart, holding the lines in one hand and eating a sandwich with the other. He finally had an appetite. Today the news had come. His father was safe, but his grandmother was dead. Now Angelina felt happy for her brother, and guilty for letting her mother die alone. She cursed herself for not going back home and forcing the old woman to emigrate. But with her brother coming home, Angelina had come to life. She promised to cook a big meal, and this was reason enough for Franco to hurry home.

He was angry that Pascuzzo hadn't closed the bakery for even one day in honor of Nonna's death. When the suggestion was made, the uncle looked at Angelina as if she were crazy. He didn't care what other Italians did. The bread business was competitive. Too many tenements had brick ovens in their basements. Day-old bread markets had sprung up everywhere. Housewives were selling their extra bread on the street.

Angelina hadn't fought Pascuzzo on this question. Both were worried about their livelihood. The boarding house, which flooded in the basement every time it rained, and which no longer sat on its timber posts but on its very walls, was scheduled for demolition by the city. The aunt and uncle would have to get back their investment by selling the land under the building. They would have to relocate, and this was a subject of long discussions.

Holding the lines between his knees, Franco wrapped the sandwich in some newspaper and put it away. He was approaching Canal Street. He shook the lines and cut the horse with his whip. The result was a desultory canter, then a return to a slow trot. Franco whipped it again. The horse didn't respond. He whipped it harder. The horse shook its head and tried to buck, but was restrained by the harness. Franco applied the whip once more and the horse sprang forward into the Canal Street traffic, weaving through pushcarts, wagons, and other horses frightened by the noisy motor cars with their trails of exhaust.

He kept the pace by whipping the horse every time it slowed. He whipped out of relief, joy, and sadness. His father was home, his grandmother gone. The wrecking of the store on the West Side and the disappearances of both his father and Carmelo could only have meant his father's death. The body could have been anywhere: in the river, in the forests of upstate New York where gangsters buried their victims. Now Franco saw that Angelina's apparent lack of concern for her brother's absence was not hardness toward death but her way of saying that she'd known something. Upon receiving the news of Nonna's death she confided that Santo had been in Sicily working for Joe Petrosino, the famous detective shot dead in Palermo.

Franco turned into the Italian section. People were already mourning Petrosino. Black bunting hung over the storefronts. Black bordered notices were pasted on the buildings. The Italian newspapers ran banner headlines: *PETROSINO UCCISO A PALERMO*. Killed in Palermo. The detective had been gunned down in the Piazza Marina, not far from Strufolino's candy factory and the Hotel *Venezia*. Preparations for a parade in his honor had been going on for weeks. The detective's body had arrived that morning. There'd been a funeral procession from the Battery to city hall. The detective lay in a closed casket in a hearse covered with flowers.

The death of a prominent Italian would have meant little to Franco. Some part of Little Italy was always celebrating the death of someone or other, usually an unremarkable person who'd gotten to L'America early enough to make a fortune. But the first news of Petrosino's assassination—on the front pages of all the city newspapers—had so frightened Angelina that she told Franco of his father's whereabouts. He was working for Petrosino in exchange for his freedom.

The news of what his father had done was bursting to be told, but Franco had so far managed to hold it in, as he held in so much else. Family secrets were just that, secrets, and no other person could be told. But now he felt a great release, a desire to tell all, to the men at the stable, to his friends on Catherine Street. Now he needn't worry about having to kill Carmelo someday, an act that haunted him much more than his part in Nicolo's death. But now that his father was alive, and famous in a secret way, Franco's life had a clarity that didn't exist when the family was broken up. His father had been an advisor to the famous Petrosino, who hadn't been smart enough to stay alive, as Franco's father had done. By now Franco had heard the account of Petrosino's death: murdered outside a restaurant where he'd been eating, shot with four bullets, three in quick succession, then a fourth. This would have been the bullet in his head, which ensured death. Several men had been arrested, including Paolo Nerone. All were released for lack of evidence. There was no mention of his father in any of the newspaper accounts: this showed how well he'd handled himself.

The horse looked back with one dark, alarmed eye and let up the pace. It was a strong, smart animal, able to withstand considerable beating when it didn't feel like working. Now Franco cut it hard once more. Nothing happened. It was used to Pascuzzo, who was much too gentle. Franco cut harder and the horse responded. The old wagon bounced and clattered over the cobblestones, which were slippery with deposits of ash and manure, treacherous with holes which could break a wagon shaft or a horse's leg.

He turned north on Elizabeth Street, slowing the pace to negotiate the pedestrians and other traffic. There was a chance that his father was home at this very minute.

"Franchino! Franchino!"

Angelina waited on the street. "He's back," she said, reaching up to take Franco's hand and rub it with both of hers. "He wants to know about your sister. He wants to know where she lives."

"Why?"

"I think he wants to talk, to make up." Her eyes were great, serious globes of eyes, and they fixed upon him with this message: You're the man now, and you must decide what to do.

Franco looked at the street ahead of him, thinking how strange that after all the trouble between them—the theft of money, leaving the house—Angelina would still want to protect her niece.

"Do you know where to find her?" she asked, but she knew the answer. "Then go and tell her that her father wants to see her today."

Franco took the cart to the boarding house and left it by the bulkhead door. There was time before the afternoon delivery to run to Drushkin's shop. If Mariana wasn't ready to reconcile with her father, he would have to tell him that. If his father demanded to know Mariana's whereabouts, he would defend his sister by pleading ignorance.

CHAPTER 41

Mariana waited outside the glow of a gas lamp and held a bundle of Drushkin's aprons near her face to protect herself. She would observe her father from behind the bundle. If he looked angry, she would back away and run through the alleys.

For the purpose of living together she'd taken Gennaro's last name, Vitale. She wore a simple wedding band to complete the deception. She was glad they hadn't married. He was finding fault already. He barked orders. He questioned every penny she spent. He threw plates against the wall when frustrated about their lack of sex. He sulked when she was tired. She would try a little longer, but leave him if necessary. There were Italian girls at Drushkin's who would gladly take a room with her.

A horse-drawn cab stopped in front of her. Her father stepped out and came toward her, hat low over his eyes, age lines beginning to frame his mouth. His arms opened to her tentatively. She backed away instinctively, but the look in his eye brought her forward again. Now the bundle of aprons came between them. Perhaps offended now, he offered his cheek. She brushed it with her lips. The wall lifted part way.

She was afraid to ask what had happened. She knew his store had been wrecked and that he'd been beaten. She wasn't sure whether this trouble resulted from her visit to the butcher shop or not. She knew that after being beaten by Petrosino's men he'd gone to Sicily, either to escape or for some secret work. According to Franco, this work was the price for his freedom, the price for the family name. Her father would offer her that name tonight. What would she do then?

His arm went around her shoulders and swept her along. Her heart fluttered, excited, afraid. He guided her into a small restaurant where a pot of coffee warmed on a stove. The counter was crowded with platters of prepared meats, vegetables, spaghetti with dry, crusted tomato sauce. The old woman who did the cooking seemed to recognize Santo but no greeting was exchanged.

Mariana faced him from across a table. He was solemn, but not angry. She kept her silence while he spoke about New Orleans.

"There was a story that I killed a boss down there. It isn't true."
He wrapped both hands around his coffee cup and looked into it.

Mariana noticed that his hands no longer had the hard, leathery
look of his Sicilian days. Looking at those hands, at the strong but
smooth fingers, Mariana knew what kind of work her father did
only to this extent: there was a society of smart men in the city who
understood that those working for a daily wage were slaves who made
others rich. In some capacity, her father worked with these men. She
therefore didn't know whether to believe his denial or not.

He continued to talk from behind the cup, calmly, evenly, as if
this were a meeting between men of affairs. But he was speaking of
dreams, little dreams, a home, possible marriage to a Sicilian woman
from a state called Arkansas, that woman now in New York, a *grosseria*
downstairs from their flat.

"Will you come and live with me?"

She didn't answer. He enlarged the picture: spacious rooms, a
public school for learning English, and a job with Franco in the new
store. Now would she come back?

Still she didn't answer.

He set down his cup and leaned forward. "Are you in trouble?"

"No."

"If you have any trouble, I'm here to help you."

She looked away. "I can't go with you."

"Why not?"

She lacked the courage to answer, and she'd lost the desire to hurt
him, that desire she'd nursed so long when she lived on Elizabeth
Street. He'd been through something that changed him.

"What are you thinking?" he asked.

"That I'm afraid of you. I never know what you're going to do."

"Listen to me. If there was one rule I lived by, it was this: to never
reveal my position completely to anyone. It was a bad rule."

She looked at him, puzzled he would say this. "But I always tried
to behave as you did."

"And this is why you can't come with me, or even tell me why not?"

Not knowing how to answer, she watched him swirl his cup, as if
the answer to a great question could be found inside it.

He said, "Do you know that you saved my life?"

"How?"

"By going to Carmelo. This took greater courage than we need right now to speak openly with each other."

Was he telling the truth about her courage? Or was he deceiving her to break down her defenses and bring her home. She turned over his remark. Since the moment they'd sat down, there'd been no trace of his former animosity. Something had happened to him in Sicily.

She said, "I went to Carmelo because I was ashamed of what I'd done, not because I had courage."

"You just didn't see your courage."

She had more questions, but each one was a risk, taking her to a higher, more precarious place. She'd never felt the right to question him before.

"Why did you go back home?" she asked.

"I had no choice."

She watched him handle the coffee cup nervously. This wasn't the same man. This man was telling her a story, step-by-step. "Death passed me by. I was close to men whose beliefs are their passions and who kill for them. But something saved me, some piece of luck, as if our misfortune from home had returned in opposite form. When they killed the detective, I was on my way to meet him."

She looked around cautiously. "Were you afraid?"

"Of course!"

She was back in that high, precarious place, where such words and attitudes had never been. "I was afraid too," she said. "With Nicolo."

"You were brave," he said. "Very brave. I should have told you that before." He glanced around the room, then leaned toward her. "What matters is that we owe each other nothing. Now will you come home with me?"

"I can't."

"Why not?"

She wanted to say the words, that she was living with Gennaro. She'd taken the wedding band off before this meeting. She was still afraid of her father's wrath, afraid of the hand coming across the table to hit her, afraid of the bitterness that would flow when he learned there was no end to her dishonor. She looked up from the circle of dried coffee in her cup. His eyes now appraised her with something of his old, dominating look.

"Speak to me," he said.

She said, "Give me time to think. Then we'll talk again."

They left the restaurant together, and once in the street they went in opposite directions. A few blocks from the restaurant she tightened her shawl against the cold. Had her father really changed? Or was his new attitude one more way of hiding his true feelings, of living up to the principle he'd always lived by: never to reveal himself.

Heading home, she breathed the cold air deeply, as she'd done on feast night in Castellano to quench the hot feeling of guilt. Oh, she had dreams! Ridiculous dreams of owning that butcher shop with Nicolo. Dreams of being a worldly-wise advisor to peasants, one who could see into the soul of any adversary. This pain she now felt was the price for this wisdom. She was learning how to discard her dreams for new ones, and to gain something in the process, as Drushkin knew how to get the most from every square inch of cloth.

She hugged the bundle of aprons. She knew the world worked bit by bit. That was how she'd worked up the courage to kill Nicolo, by letting the shame ferment in her breast. She'd hidden the pistol in a pile of laundry by the gate. On the first day he passed by, she didn't have the courage to go near it. On the second day she pulled out the pistol but her hand shook so badly that she couldn't raise it. On the third day she was more frightened than ever, so weak her knees almost buckled. She was ready to give up her idea of revenge. But then Nicolo's eyes flickered under the hat brim, as if their game could begin again even though he was married. The insult was too much to bear. She waited for him to pass, took out the pistol, and raised it high enough to rest on the crossbar of the gate. She pulled the trigger just as the weapon began to chatter against the iron.

She was American now. She carried her night work home: four dozen aprons including buttons and thread. She would earn one penny per apron and tell Gennaro her pay was half that amount. She would turn pennies into dollars and sew them into her coat. Then she would look for a better job, and a better place to live, alone. A new life would take shape. Things could always change in L'America.

She lowered her head and walked into the wind, resisting it.

ACKNOWLEDGMENTS

I am indebted to those who came before me, writers who captured the immigrant experience and its foundation in Mediterranean history. I learned much from Italian-American writers such as di Donato, Fante, and Puzo, who spoke of the culture as it mixed, or did not mix, with American ways. Storytellers and historians from Homer and Herodotus to Virgil and Plutarch also validated the world I was writing about. I was helped by the Italians as well, Moravia, Morante, Pasolini, Sciascia, and Dolci, writers who also placed my characters in context. Some of the stories folded into *Sicilian Dreams* were told by my grandparents, aunts and uncles, those closer to what is now called the diaspora. Other stories were drawn from firsthand accounts of the immigrant experience discovered at The Center for Migration Studies in Staten Island.

There are also friends who read my work and with whom I could commiserate and celebrate: the late David Calicchio, Chard deNiord, David Rohn, Laurette Folk, Reginald Martell, Nell Lasch, and Jerry Carbone to name a few, all helping hands. Copy editors Justyn Moulds and Eliani Torres helped lift the fog; my wife and Muse, Susan Sichel, and all in my extended family—including three sisters and four children—provided essential support. Two other spirits are present when I sit down to work: one is the late William Price Fox, the Iowa Workshop mentor who taught me not only how to work, but how to read. The other is my Sicilian grandmother, Petrina Giaimo who supplemented her poor steamship fare with homemade *capponatina* during her passage. She also told me the story of the woman back in her little town who tried to kill her lover but the pistol backfired. When I said that I wanted to be a writer, Petrina cleared a space in the furnace room in Queens and told everyone in the house to be quiet.

To all these and more.

Marlboro, Vermont, 2020

ABOUT THE AUTHOR

VINCENT PANELLA is the author of the memoir, *The Other Side, Growing up Italian in America*. His novel, *Cutter's Island*, about an incident in the early life of Julius Caesar, received a ForeWord award, and was called by author Steven Pressfield, ". . . a perfect flawless gem." He is a Pushcart nominee in short fiction, and Primo Magazine said of his story collection, *Lost Hearts*, that it ". . .calls to be included in every Italian-American's library." Vincent is a graduate of the Iowa Writer's Workshop and the former Writing Specialist at Vermont Law School. He grew up in Queens and lives in Marlboro, Vermont with his wife, Susan Sichel.

VIA Folios
A refereed book series dedicated to the culture of Italians and Italian Americans.